JUN 2017

AUG 2017

ELLE

PHILIPPE DJIAN

D0189309

ALSO A FILM BY PAUL VERHOEVEN

A SONY PICTURES CLASSICS RELEASE SAÏD BEN SAÏD and MICHEL MERKT present ISABELLE HUPPERT "ELLE" A PAUL VERHOEVEN film
LAURENT LAFITTE from the comédie-française ANNE CONSIGNY CHARLES BERLING VIRGINIE EFIRA with JUDITH MAGRE CHRISTIAN BERKEL
JONAS BLOQUET ALICE ISAAZ VIMALA PONS ARTHUR MAZET RAPHAEL LENGLET LUCAS PRISOR music by ANNE DUDLEY
A FRENCH-GERMAN co-production SBS PRODUCTIONS TWENTY TWENTY VISION FILMPRODUKTION FRANCE 2 CINÉMA
IN CO-PRODUCTION WITH ENTRE CHIEN ET LOUP and PROXIMUS with the participation of CANAL + FRANCE TÉLÉVISIONS
OCS CENTRE NATIONAL DU CINÉMA ET DE L'IMAGE ANIMÉE and the GERMAN FEDERAL FILM BOARD – FFA
WITH THE SUPPORT OF TAX SHELTER DU GOUVERNEMENT FEDERAL BELGE CASA KAFKA PICTURES BELFIUS
AND THE SUPPORT OF CINÉMAGE 7 DEVELOPPEMENT CO-PRODUCED BY THANASSIS KARATHANOS KATE MERKT DIANA ELBAUM
SÉBASTIEN DELLOYE FRANÇOIS TOUWAIDE PRODUCED BY SAÏD BEN SAÏD and MICHEL MERKT SCREENPLAY BY DAVID BIRKE
BASED ON THE NOVEL "OH..." BY PHILIPPE DJIAN © PHILIPPE DJIAN ET ÉDITIONS GALLIMARD 2012 DIRECTED BY PAUL VERHOEVEN
COPYRIGHT PHOTO : © 2015 GUY FERRANDIS / SBS PRODUCTIONS
© 2015 SBS PRODUCTIONS – SBS FILMS – TWENTY TWENTY VISION FILMPRODUKTION – FRANCE 2 CINÉMA – ENTRE CHIEN ET LOUP
WWW.ELLEMOVIE.COM   WWW.SONYCLASSICS.COM

WWW.SONYCLASSICS.COM
SONY PICTURES CLASSICS

ELLE

PHILIPPE DJIAN

TRANSLATED FROM THE FRENCH BY
MICHAEL KATIMS

OTHER PRESS
NEW YORK

Copyright © Philippe Djian et Éditions Gallimard, Paris, 2012

Originally published in French as "*Oh…*" in 2012 by Éditions Gallimard, Paris

English translation copyright © Michael Katims, 2017

Excerpt from "A Piece of News" from *A Curtain of Green and Other Stories* by Eudora Welty. Copyright © 1941 and renewed 1969 by Eudora Welty. Reprinted by permission of Houghton Mifflin Harcourt Publishing Company. All rights reserved.

Production editor: Yvonne E. Cárdenas
Text designer: Julie Fry
This book was set in Swift and Quicksand.

10 9 8 7 6 5 4 3 2 1

Library of Congress Cataloging-in-Publication Data
Names: Djian, Philippe, 1949– author. | Katims, Michael, translator.
Title: Elle : a novel / Philippe Djian ; translated from the French by Michael Katims.
Other titles: "Oh…". English
Description: New York : Other Press, 2017. | "Originally published in France
    as "Oh…" by Editions Gallimard, Paris, in 2012"—Title page verso.
Identifiers: LCCN 2017008081 (print) | LCCN 2017012999 (ebook) |
    ISBN 9781590519165 (e-book) | ISBN 9781590519158 (paperback)
Subjects: LCSH: Divorced women—France—Fiction. | Television producers
    and directors—France—Paris—Fiction. | Sexual abuse victims—Fiction. |
    BISAC: FICTION / Media Tie-In. | FICTION / Contemporary Women. | GSAFD:
    Mystery fiction.
Classification: LCC PQ2664.J5 (ebook) | LCC PQ2664.J5 O313 2017 (print) |
    DDC 843/.914—dc23
LC record available at https://lccn.loc.gov/2017008081

Publisher's note:
This is a work of fiction. Names, characters, places, and incidents either are the product of the author's imagination or are used fictitiously, and any resemblance to actual persons, living or dead, events, or locales is entirely coincidental.

It was dark and vague outside.
The storm had rolled away to faintness
like a wagon crossing a bridge.

—EUDORA WELTY, "A PIECE OF NEWS"

I MUST HAVE SCRAPED MY CHEEK. It burns. My jaw hurts. I knocked a vase over when I fell, I remember hearing it shatter on the floor and I'm wondering if I got cut with a piece of glass. I don't know. The sun is still shining outside. The weather's good. Little by little, I catch my breath. I feel an awful migraine coming on, any minute.

Two days ago, as I was watering my garden, an unsettling message appeared to me when I looked up to the sky. A cloud, with an unmistakably distinct shape. I looked around, wondering if it were intended for someone else, but I didn't see anyone. And there was no sound either, just me watering. Not a word, not a scream, not a whisper of air, not a single motor—and God knows there is no shortage of mowers and blowers around here.

Generally, I can feel it when the outside world cuts in. I've been known to stay holed up for several days in a row, never setting foot outdoors, if I perceive some unsettling omen in the erratic flight of a bird—coupled with a shrill cry or some sinister croaking—or if some weird ray of sunlight makes its way through the branches and hits me right in the face, or if I lean over to give a few coins to a man sitting on the sidewalk and he suddenly grabs my arm and shouts in my face, "The demons! The demons with their demon faces! I threaten to kill them and then they obey!" The man belched, kept repeating this same sentence over and over with crazy eyes, never letting me go, and when I got home that night I canceled my train ticket, immediately forgetting all about the reason for my trip, finding it suddenly and completely unimportant. You see, I'm neither suicidal nor deaf to the warnings, messages, and signs that I receive.

When I was sixteen, I missed a plane after a night of drinking at the Bayonne Festival and the plane crashed. I thought about this for a long time. Then and there, I decided I would take certain precautions to protect my life. I accepted the fact that these things exist and anyone who chose to laugh it off, well, I just let them laugh. I'm not sure why, but I've always felt that the signs in the sky are the most telling ones, the most urgent. An X-shaped cloud — rare enough that it gets my full attention — would normally put me on high alert, every time. I don't know what happened. How could I have dropped my guard? Of course it's a little (or a lot?) to do with Marty. I'm so ashamed. I'm so furious now. Furious at myself. There's a chain on my door. There's a goddamn chain on my door. Did I just forget? I stand up and go put it on. I briefly pinch my lower lip between my teeth, I hold still for a full minute. Apart from the broken vase, I can't see any mess. I go upstairs to change. Vincent is coming for dinner with his girlfriend, and nothing is ready.

The young woman is pregnant, but it isn't Vincent's child. I have stopped talking about that. I have nothing to gain. I don't have the strength to fight him anymore. Or the will. Once I figured out how much he takes after his father, I thought I would lose my mind. Her name is Josie. She's looking for an apartment for Vincent and herself, and for the baby on the way. Richard pretended to be sick when he heard the price of Paris rentals. He paced up and down muttering to himself. He's made a habit of that now. I can see how much older he's grown, just how somber these twenty years have made him. "You mean monthly or yearly?" he asked, putting on that mean look of his. He wasn't sure he could swing it. As for me, I'm supposed to have a regular and generous income.

Naturally.

"You wanted a son," I tell him. "Remember?"

I left him because he became unbearable, and now he's more unbearable than ever. I tell him he should take up smoking again, or jogging. Anything to get rid of that bitterness which drives him most of the time.

"Excuse me, but go fuck yourself," he tells me. "Anyway, I'm broke right now. I thought he got a job?"

"I don't know, talk it over with him."

I don't have the will to fight him either. I spent more than twenty years of my life with this man, but sometimes I wonder how I ever found the strength.

I run a bath. My cheek is red and maybe a little yellow as well, like pottery, and there's a tiny drop of blood at the corner of my lip. My hair is truly a mess. The clip I was wearing let a lot of it loose. I pour some bath salts into the tub. This is madness because it's already five o'clock and the girl, Josie…I don't know her very well. I don't know what to think of her.

Yet there is an incredibly warm and beautiful light, so removed from the slightest whisper of a threat. It's so hard for me to believe that something like this could happen to me under a sky so blue, on such a gorgeous day. The bathroom is awash with sunlight. I can hear cries in the distance, far-off children playing. A dusting of clouds on the horizon. Birds, squirrels, and so on.

It feels so good. This bath is a miracle. I close my eyes. I can't say I've wiped it all away, but after a moment, I'm completely back to myself. The expected migraine has not come. I order sushi from the place that delivers.

I've known worse with men I freely chose.

After picking up the larger pieces of the vase, I vacuum the spot where I fell. Just to think, only hours before I had been lying there, my heart pounding. It makes me pretty uncomfortable. And right as I'm about to pour myself a drink, I get a message from Irène, my mother, who is seventy-five and whom I haven't seen — or heard from — in a month. She says she had a dream about me, that I was calling her for help. But I didn't call her at all.

Vincent doesn't seem quite convinced by my story. "Your bicycle is in excellent shape," he says. "Isn't that odd?" I stare at him a moment, then I shrug my shoulders. Josie is bright red. Vincent has just grabbed her wrist, hard, and forced her to release the peanuts. Apparently, she's already gained forty pounds.

They don't look right together. Richard, who wouldn't know, told me that kind of girl could be good in bed. What does that mean, to be *good in bed*? In the meantime, she wants a nine-hundred-square-foot two-bedroom in a certain neighborhood. Nothing that size can be found for less than three thousand euros.

"I filled out an application at McDonald's," Vincent says. "For the meantime."

I encourage him in this endeavor, or something better for his self-esteem—why not? A pregnant woman is expensive to keep.

"You should know..." I started to say, before he even introduced her to me. "I'm not asking what you think," he answered. "I don't give a shit what you think."

That's how he acts with me since I left his father. Richard is an excellent tragic actor. And Vincent is his best audience. As we're finishing dinner, he looks at me again with suspicious eyes. "What is it with you? What's wrong?" I can't stop thinking about it, of course. Throughout the meal, it was never far away. I'm wondering if I were chosen at random or if I had been followed, if it's someone I know. Their talk of rent and the baby's bedroom doesn't interest me at all, though I admire what they're taking on—what they're attempting—a trick by which their problem becomes my problem. I stare at him for a second, trying to imagine his expression if I told him what happened to me this afternoon. But it is no longer in my repertoire. I no longer have the power to imagine my son's reactions.

"Did you get into a fight?"

"A fight, Vincent?" I let out a small chortle. "A fight?"

"Did you slug it out with someone?"

"Oh, come on, don't be stupid. I'm not in the habit of 'slugging it out' with people."

I get up and leave, joining Josie on the veranda. It's a fine, cool evening, but she is still fanning herself because it's so oppressive. Those last few weeks are the hardest. You couldn't get me to go through that again. I'd have cut my own belly open to put an end to the agony. Vincent knows that. I never tried to gloss that over. I always wanted him to know. And never to forget. My mother told me the same thing and it didn't kill me.

We stare into the starry black sky. I watch Josie out of the corner of my eye. I've only seen her half a dozen times and I don't know much about her. She's perfectly likable, actually. Knowing my son Vincent, I pity her. But there's something stony about her, something cool and stubborn. She would do just fine if she made an effort. She's solid, I can feel it. There's something lurking inside her.

"So you're due in December? Getting closer."

"He's right," she answers. "You're all upset."

"No, I'm not," I say. "Not at all. What does he know about me?"

I close the door behind them. I make my rounds of the ground floor, carrying a meat cleaver. I check the doors and the windows. I shut myself up in my room. When dawn starts to filter in, I haven't slept a wink. Morning grows blue, resplendent. I rush off to see my mother. As I enter her living room, there is a young, athletic, though altogether ordinary man on his way out.

I wonder if my aggressor from the night before looked like him. All I can remember is a ski mask with two holes for the eyes, and I can't even remember if it was blue or red. I can't remember if he looked like this self-satisfied person who winks at me as he leaves my mother's apartment.

"Mom, how much are you paying them? How demeaning!" I say. "Can't you go out with a professor or a writer for a change? I mean, do you really need some stud? At your age."

"This can't touch me. I have nothing to be ashamed about, it's my sex life. You're just a little bitch. Your father's right."

"Mom, stop it. Don't talk to me about him, he's fine where he is."

"What are you talking about? You silly girl, your father is definitely not fine where he is. He's going insane."

"He *is* insane. Ask his psychiatrist."

She gives me breakfast. I think she's had something redone since the last time. Or just Botoxed maybe, I don't know. She has changed her life completely since her husband (who unfortunately is also my father) got put away, though at first she did fight the good fight. A real slut. She has spent a lot of money on cosmetic surgery over the last couple of years. Sometimes, in a certain light, she frightens me.

"Fine. What do you want?"

"What do I want? Mom, you called me."

She looks at me for a moment, with no reaction.

Then she leans over toward me and says, "Think it over before you speak. Weigh your answer. What would you say if I got remarried? Think."

"It's simple, I'd kill you. No need to think it over."

She shakes her head slowly, crosses her legs, lights a cigarette.

"You've always wanted some sanitized version of life. All that is dark or abnormal...it's always scared you silly."

"I would kill you. Spare me the psychobabble. You've been warned."

I had my eyes closed up until then. Of course her sexual appetite has always surprised me, I would even say disgusted me, and I don't approve. But I decided to be open-minded about it. If that's how she gets by, I can accept it, though I don't want the details. Fine. On the other hand, if things get too serious and venture out onto uncertain terrain, as is the case with this marriage stuff, well, I just have to step in. Who's the lucky guy this time? Who's the one she met? And who exactly is this Ralf—the son of a gun has a name—who shows up in the frame and casts a shadow over everything?

I eliminated a lawyer who said he was crazy about her by telling him she was carrying a virus, then a branch manager by revealing the truth about us—which kills the mood as well—and they hadn't even proposed.

I don't think I could put up with such a twisted thing. A seventy-five-year-old woman. The ceremony, the flowers, the honeymoon. She looks like one of those terrifying old actresses—completely plastered over, breast-lift at five thousand a pair, eyes all agleam, tanned to the hilt.

"I'd like to know who is going to pay my rent in the years to come," she finally says with a sigh. "I'd like to know, tell me."

"I will, of course. Haven't I always?" She smiles, but she's obviously very put out.

"You are so selfish, Michèle. It's frightening."

I butter the toast that has just popped up in the toaster. I haven't seen her in more than a month and I'm already ready to leave.

"What if something happened to you?" she asks. I feel like telling her that's just a chance we'll have to take.

I cover one slice of toast with raspberry jam. I slather it on. On purpose. It's hard not to get it all over my fingers, and I hand it to her. She hesitates. It looks like lumps of blood. She stares at the thing for a moment and then she says, "I think he's not long for this world, Michèle. I think you should know. Your father is not long for this world."

"Well, good riddance. That's all I have to say."

"You don't have to be so callous, you know. Don't do something that you'll regret for the rest of your life."

"What? What would I regret? Are you delirious?"

"He paid his debt. He's been in prison for thirty years. That's a faraway memory."

"I wouldn't say so. I don't think it's far away. How could you say such a horrible thing? You think it's far away? You want binoculars?" There are tears welling in my eyes, like I'd just swallowed a teaspoon of Dijon mustard. "I have no intention of going, Mom. I have no intention of going there. Make no mistake about that. He's been dead to me for a very long time."

She gives me a sidelong glance, full of blame, then turns toward the window. "I don't even know if he still recognizes me. But he does ask for you."

"Oh, really? And what do I care? What am I supposed to feel? And since when are you his messenger?"

"Don't wait. That's all I have to say. Don't wait."

"Listen, I'm never going to set foot in that prison. There is no chance of me visiting him. He's starting to fade from my memory and I would like him to completely disappear, if that's possible."

"How can you say such a thing? That's a terrible thing to say."

"Oh, spare me, would you please? Please. That monster ruined our lives, didn't he?"

"It wasn't all bad. He wasn't all evil, far from it. You know that very well. You might muster a little pity."

"Pity? Mom, take a good look at me. I don't have any pity for him. Not for one second. I hope he expires right where he is, and I will certainly not go see him. Forget it."

She doesn't know that I see him in dreams. Or more precisely, I see his outline, that electric darkness, in the shadows. I can make out his head and shoulders, but I can't tell if he's facing me, looking at me, or if he has his back turned. He seems to be sitting down. He's not talking to me. He's waiting. And when I awake, I still have that image in my mind. That shadow.

I can't help thinking that there may be some relationship between the attack I have just endured and my father's actions—just as we always wonder, my mother and I, each time we go through some ordeal. We wonder because we experienced it, we were on the receiving end of more than our share of spitting and blows, just because we were his wife and his daughter. Overnight we had lost all our relationships, all our neighbors, all our friends. As if we bore the mark on our foreheads.

We experienced the anonymous phone calls, got called names in the middle of the night, received the obscene letters through the mail, our trash cans spilled outside our door, the words scrawled on the walls, the pushing and shoving at the post office, the small humiliations in the shops, the shattered windows. Nothing can surprise me now. No one could swear that all the embers have been snuffed out, that there isn't someone in a corner somewhere cooking up the next thing that might befall us. How could we believe in chance?

That very night, I get a text. "I thought you were really tight, for a woman of your age. But hey." I fall over backward, breathless. I read it two or three times, then I answer: "Who are you?" But there is no reply.

I spend my morning and part of my afternoon reading screenplays. They are piling up on my desk. Maybe there's a clue to be found in that as well, I think, some young writer I shot down and who hates me more than anything.

On the way, I stopped at the gun shop and got myself some red-pepper spray cans, for the eyes. The small size is very practical and can be used several times. I used to use it all the time when I was younger. I was very quick and I had no fears about taking public transportation. I was very agile. I had learned over the years. I know how to dodge someone, I could run pretty fast, I could get around the block in under two minutes. That's no longer the case. That's over. But fortunately, I no longer have any reason to run. I could even take up smoking again. Who would care?

I put aside my dreary reading in midafternoon.

There is nothing worse than that feeling of stupidly wasted time when you close a bad script. One of them flies across the room where I work and lands in an extra-large trash can exclusively reserved for that purpose. Sometimes that wasted time is painful. Sometimes it gets so bad you want to cry. At about five p.m., I think of my rapist again because at that time, forty-eight hours earlier, he used the fact that I was busy with Marty in order to burst through my door like some demonic jack-in-the-box.

Then all at once I realize he must have been watching me. Waiting for the right moment. Watching me. And for a moment I just sit there, speechless.

I go into the office, check my mail, my phone messages. I make a few calls, delegate a few tasks. Anna comes to talk to me, and toward the end of the conversation, she says, "I got to say it, you don't look right."

I act like I can't get over it: "Don't be silly! I mean, just look at this gorgeous day, all this sunshine!"

She smiles. Anna would probably be the right person to talk to, if I decide to talk. We've known each other for so long. But something is preventing me. This thing with her husband?

I go to the gynecologist. I do the necessary tests.

Vincent calls me to ask if I would at least cosign the lease. I am silent for a few seconds.

"You were so unkind to me, Vincent."

"Yeah, I know. Shit, I'm sorry. I know."

"I can't give you that money, Vincent. I'm trying to build a retirement fund. I don't want to depend on you later on. I don't want you to pay my way. I won't be a burden."

"All right, I get it. Mom. At least cosign the fucking lease."

"Don't just come to me when you want something."

I can hear him smashing the receiver against something. As a small boy he already had a temper. Just like his father.

"Mom, would you please just fucking say yes or no."

"Stop saying 'fuck.' What kind of talk is that?"

We make an appointment with the landlord. Economic uncertainty and stagnation have reached such proportions that a simple transaction like renting an apartment has become an outpouring of mutual distrust. Birth certificate, driver's license, pay slips, certificates, photocopies, promissory notes, papers, handwritten letters, religion, and countless other precautions on the part of the lessor in order to protect against the chaos that may follow. I ask if it's a joke, but it's not.

On his way out, Vincent says he wants to buy me a drink and we go into a bar. He orders a Hawaiian beer and a glass of South African dry white wine. We toast the fact that he is now the proud tenant of a six-hundred-square-foot three-room apartment with southern exposure and a small balcony, for which I have cosigned the lease.

"You realize what this means, Vincent. You have to step up. If you don't pay your rent it will fall to me, and I won't be able to keep it up for long. Are you listening to me? This is not a game, Vincent. And I'm not only worried about you. I'm also thinking of myself and of your grandmother, whose rent I also pay, as you know. Vincent, they are very uptight nowadays. They won't let you get away with anything. They can have your account frozen in no time, sue you, and the court costs would be entirely yours to cover. They will send assessors to inventory your possessions. They will humiliate you, and that's not all. Always keep in mind that men who speculate on rice and wheat already have so much blood on their hands, they're not worried about spilling a little more."

He looks me over a moment, then smiles. "I've changed, but you don't see it."

I would love to believe him. I would love to take him in my arms and smother him with grateful kisses. But I'll wait and see.

There's a meeting in my office. There are about fifteen of them. It's been a few months now since we started having these fairly tense weekly meetings, because their work is worthless ever since they got back from vacation. Nothing original or powerful in the slightest has been suggested to me and, once I've given them high praise and expressed my unbridled admiration for their exceptional writing talent, their downcast faces disgust me.

There are about ten men. Perhaps he is among them. Perhaps I denigrated one person's work in particular without even realizing it because everything I read blurs into a mass of mediocrity. But I don't notice anything. Not one glance I could truly say belonged to the man who blithely violated me. Not long ago, I was still certain that, even if he kept his mask on, I could spot him if I were around him, that my entire body would start shivering, that my entire being would bristle. Now I'm not so sure.

When everyone gets up to leave, I go out with them, mixing with them, brushing past them on purpose in the narrow hallway, vaguely apologizing for the accidental contact. But I can feel nothing. I recognize no smell, no cologne as I pass discreetly from one to the next, exhorting them to give me the best of themselves next week if they're interested in keeping their jobs—and no one kids around with that anymore—but otherwise no, I don't feel a thing, not even the slightest spark.

I finally speak to Richard about it. About my appalling misadventure. He goes pale, then he gets up to pour himself a drink.

"Do you think I'm especially tight?" I ask him.

He lets out a long sigh and sits down next to me, shaking his head. Then he takes my hand in both of his and doesn't say another word.

If ever I had deep feelings for a man, it was for Richard. And I did marry him. Even now, through the little things—like when he takes my hand or tries to meet my eyes with just a hint of worry, when from within an ocean of mutual incompatibilities some tiny islands of affection still emerge, some pure understanding—I can still clearly perceive the echo of what we meant to one another during those few years.

Aside from that, we hate each other. Well, he hates me. His inability to sell his screenplays and his having to stoop to working on horrible television movies and stomach-wrenching TV programs, with assholes, is apparently partially my fault. I don't do the right thing, if you listen to him. I have never lifted a finger, never made use of my relationships. Right from the start, I've been totally, lamentably going through the motions and yada yada. No one gets out of this alive. The breach gets wider and wider.

I'm unable to write a screenplay myself. I don't have that talent. But I know how to recognize a good one when I see it, and I have nothing to prove in that respect. I'm well known for it. If Anna Vangerlove weren't my friend, I'd have already sold out to the Chinese and their freaking head-hunters. It just so happens that Richard has never written a good screenplay, and I should know. I should know all too well, I guess.

"I wouldn't say you're tight," he blurts, "and I wouldn't say you're not tight either. You're somewhere in between, as far as I can make out."

There is a message hanging in the air, but I don't want to sleep with him now. We have allowed ourselves the odd parenthetical tumble, but this is rare. Wanting to at the same time doesn't happen every day after twenty years in each other's lives.

I look at him and shrug. Sometimes holding a hand is not enough—this man still has a lot to learn.

He stares at me with a sort of grimace. "I didn't get scabies," I say with a chuckle. Now I wish he would leave. The sun is setting and the leaves all lit up. "It might have been much worse. I wasn't crippled or disfigured."

"In any case, I can't get my mind around how you're taking this."

"Really? How should I take it, then, in your opinion? Would you like to see me moan and groan? Should I go off to a retreat, get some needles stuck in me, go see a shrink?"

The surroundings are silent, the sun skimming the ground, the light oozing all around. Whatever else happens, down here on earth things are still as beautiful. And so the horror is complete. Richard wasn't losing his hair when we separated, but for the last two years he sure has.

There's a little clearing on the top of his skull, glowing a gentle pink, when he bends over to kiss my fingers.

"If you've got something to ask me, Richard, do it quickly. Then leave, because I'm tired."

I go out on the veranda, to enjoy the dusk. I'm surrounded by neighbors, lights shining in the windows of their houses. Our small street is generously lit, our gardens and yards have practically no shade. But I don't go out too far, I keep my guard up. I have known that state for a long time. At first it was nearly permanent. Then it faded and largely disappeared when we moved. Being constantly aware, ready to dodge the danger—not to answer, just get out of there as quickly as possible, leaving any pursuers in the dust. I know all about it.

Hardly four days have gone by. I light a cigarette. Now I can better see how things happened. I went to open the door, in the back of the house, when I heard Marty meowing. I was wondering why that idiot cat didn't just go around to the front. I imagine the man had picked him up in order to get me outside. And that's exactly what happened. I put my book down and I went outside.

On the other hand, I have no memory of the purely sexual part of the assault. I was living with so much tension—a tension that was in actual fact the sum of all the tensions I had endured up until that moment, in trying to escape the pack of howling beasts my father had unleashed—I must have had a mental disconnect, recording nothing of the actual act. So I can't say a thing about it. I can't know how my body reacted. And I can't know what to do with this suffocating rage and fury.

I am neither torn nor bruised. I'm a little irritated, but that should go away. I don't practice anal sex at the drop of a hat, so naturally I bled a little, but that's not very serious. It's slight. I have no image of it. The content of the text message, however, the tone—that irony, that familiarity—and the derogatory turn of phrase make me think this is punishment, obviously linked either to my work or to my father's hellish deeds, delivered by some person who knows me.

Aside from my cheek, rendered presentable by a smattering of face powder and a touch of blush, I do have some ugly marks on my arms and wrists—where he pinned them with his bare hands to the ground. Enormous bracelet-shaped bruises, which I hide with long sleeves. But that's about it, thank God. At least I'm not obliged to wax poetic about the origin of an eye completely swollen closed, or a broken tooth or crutches or worse, like some more unfortunate souls. At least I can decide for myself what scope to afford what happens next, indeed if I wish anything to happen at all. In fact, I'm unable to join them. I can't fit into their vast procession. I won't wear that as a badge, as the mark of belonging to some entity. And I will not lose my position in the bargain. I have no time to be distracted. I must bring all my energy to bear. I didn't steal the job I now hold, but I have also become aware of just how tenuous it truly is in this wave of layoffs that has hit. No one is immune, anything can happen. Some turned their heads for just an instant and lost everything. There you have it.

My mother is on about my father again. She's looking at Christmastime and points out that these are probably his last lucid moments. I hang up without answering.

I go home. I lock the door behind me. I check the doors, the windows. I go up to my bedroom. Marty jumps on the bed, stretches, yawns. For home, I chose the Guardian Angel model, with the incapacitant agent. Each time you spray, six milliliters of active ingredient are blasted into the air at over one hundred mph.

I left Richard before he discovered my affair with Robert Vangerlove, because I didn't want to hurt him any more than I had to. Hurting Richard was never my intention. Actually, I think I was already so ashamed of sleeping with Anna's husband because she was—and still is—my best friend. But it was either that or die of boredom, that or hang myself. One morning, there's a Robert Vangerlove standing there, a perfectly ordinary and soulless man, a transparent man, with a slightly stupid smile on his face, and you say to yourself, "Why not?" You float. You spray yourself out in billions of indecision cells. That's how you find yourself with an affair on your hands, a white man with a nascent belly, for the most part pleasant but dull, and you have no idea how to get rid of him. All right, so he's not the worst lover in the history of the world, but there's no more to it than that.

He calls me up and he says, "Anna is away this weekend. Could we—"

I cut him off. "Robert, I'm indisposed right now."

"You are? What do you mean? I'll be around for a few days."

"I know, Robert. There's nothing I can do."

"Even with a condom?"

"Right, I'm sorry. How was your trip? Did you sell a lot of shoes?"

"The Italians are cleaning our clocks. I figure I've got another year, maybe two at the outside."

"Anyway, will you be around for the holidays? I don't know yet myself."

"I have a hard time getting away over the holidays."

"Yes, I know you have a hard time getting away over the holidays, Robert. But that doesn't matter. I know your situation. You know, I'm not a complicated person."

I hang up.

It's a miracle that nobody knows about him and me. In the course of a conversation, Anna confided to me that she had chosen an ordinary-looking man in order to have peace of mind. I made no comment.

I'd like us to remain friends if we wind up breaking it off, but to be honest, I rather doubt it. I don't really know him very well—sleeping with him didn't teach me much—but I don't think he would have a lot of time for me if I were just a friend. That's the feeling I get. Richard never had more than a lukewarm relationship with him. "How did he go about seducing her, for fuck's sake?" He asks the question regularly, especially when we're coming home from a dinner party they attended and during which he made a vain attempt at flirting with her. "Oh, listen, that's a mystery, Richard. You know that. Why do people wind up together? Look at us. It's a total mystery, right?"

That scene happened more than two years ago. One month later, we were separated and I could finally breathe. Alone at last. Free. Free from a husband whose foul mood oppressed me, free from a son whose days were filled with who knows what, and hardly even a prisoner of my affair with Robert. There was no real urgency to put an end to that.

What a revelation. As I look back on it now, I can say that solitude is the greatest gift, the only refuge.

We should have split up sooner, instead of waiting. We were performing, each for the other. We were showing our worst aspects to one another, acting like lowdown, petty, obnoxious, small-minded, lost, and capricious people, as the situation required, and we really gained nothing by it. We may have lost a little self-esteem; he says so, and I agree.

Leaving someone takes more courage than you might suppose—that is, unless you're one of those zombies with burned-out brains, those simpletons one meets on occasion. Each morning I woke up and I couldn't find the courage. And the last days all I did was moan. It took us a long time. Three days. Three long days and three long nights to tear ourselves away from one another, divvying up the furniture, the photographs, the films, the documents, the silverware.

Sure, there was some yelling. A couple of things got broken. Richard took it very hard because he felt I had picked the exact worst time to throw that in his face. Those are his words. He was pitching his project. The biggest project of his life, as he told it, the one that would catapult him squarely into the realm of the elite, especially if Leo got excited about the role. And here I come with my bullshit and I saw his legs off. Those are his words.

"Don't try to make me feel guilty, Richard. Don't start."

His answer was to slap me right across the face. I could have hugged him. "Thank you, Richard," I told him. "Thank you." Dawn had hardly broken when I got out of the taxi, handed the bag to the porter. I signed the card. I was escorted to the elevator. I smiled. I was going to sleep all alone in a king-size bed, after three days of fighting. Hallelujah. I wiped away a few tears of joy. My phone rang several times, but I didn't answer.

This morning, I'm having a meeting with a dozen writers. The rape victim has no qualms about crossing her legs good and high, compensating for the wan expression on her face. To make matters worse, I hardly slept. This is the first night when I've awakened with a start—a man on top of me, whereas I'm actually all wound up in my blanket. I bolt upright, cry out, and at that precise moment the screen on my phone lights up with a message. My heart starts beating.

The message says, low battery. It shuts off. I plug it in. The moonlight in the garden streams through the leaves like icy blood. It's three in the morning. The phone comes on again. I nibble on a nail, wait. I hear an owl hooting outside. Then the phone tells me there is no signal. I stifle a whimper, short of breath. Goddamn technology. I'm seething. How many phones are being shattered right at that instant, all over the world? Shattered on a stone wall or bursting through a window at jet-engine speed? I rise, lean out the window. The air is cool. I shiver. I hold the phone outside and, miraculously, I snag a signal. The message says, "Be ready, Michèle."

I cry out in surprise. The owl seems to answer me. Trembling, I type: "Stop this. Who are you?" I wait. No answer. I have to take something to get back to sleep.

I call a locksmith. I double up on security. I have a solid dead bolt installed on my bedroom door. When the guy winds up suggesting I have an alarm installed for the ground floor, I say yes.

With the exception of Richard, everyone is wondering what is going on with me. I tell them my insurance agent made me an offer because of the crime wave and I change the subject.

The guy spends the afternoon installing his system. There are two of them, they do test runs. I can't say if their presence is reassuring or if it actually scares the hell out of me. I wave to the couple in the house across the road. I'm telling them that I'm here and demonstrating to the two guys, there are witnesses.

I know how stupid it is, but I can't help it. They leave. They've installed a keypad that lights up near the front door. It has colored LED lights. And a video screen where you can see what's happening on the other side of the door.

I see Richard. I open the door for him.

He looks over my new system and says I made the right decision, even before I tell him about the second text message. "That's good. This is better. How are you? Have you gotten over the shock?"

I sort of shrug. How can you explain it? Especially to a man. How can you explain what it *feels* like. I give up and get some cold chicken out of the fridge, ask him if he wants some.

He says, "I'm glad it's just the two of us because I want to talk to you." I start to stiffen, tucking in my chin. Something inside me is screaming, *Oh, no! For chrissakes!* because

I know where he's going, I know what cliff he's leading us toward. I know that tone of voice. I know that furtive glance he has just darted at me, which he immediately repackages with his most winning grin. Richard believed for a long time that there was an actor inside him. Sort of a De Niro type, to hear him tell it. It needed to find expression and that's why he took classes for a whole year. I am looking at the result.

He moves away from the table, crosses his hands in his lap, hunches over, bows his head.

"Michèle, this time I'm bringing you something really solid. Believe me. And by the way, while we're on the subject, that time you turned me down you were totally right. You were right and I was wrong. I was too close to it and my pride got in the way. Let's forget about it. It's over. But thanks to you, I have come to terms with my weaknesses and I have gotten back to a piece I gave up on long ago. Which I had lost faith in. And, of course, I followed your advice. You won't be disappointed. I really went all out, no exaggeration."

He leans over as he finishes his speech and brings a plastic bag out from under the table. From out of that bag, he produces his new screenplay.

Anna doesn't think much of it. And neither do I. Richard is a bad screenwriter because, in the end, he has contempt for film. He has contempt for television as well, but he never had any stake in TV because it doesn't bring recognition, riches, and glory. When I say he has contempt for film, I mean he puts himself first. And all that is not born of sacrifice is vain. She agrees. We're having a quick lunch in a café near the center, where they make very decent club sandwiches.

She knows what this means for me and she offers to take care of it. I say thank you but no. This is mainly between Richard and me. I owe him that much. I owe him the truth. I shake my head, contemplating the enormous task ahead. One of destruction and reconstruction.

How is he going to take it this time? I'm very angry at him for bringing us here again. We both know how painful and difficult this situation is. We've been through it already, and it was the most tiresome period in my life.

How could he put us through it again? How could he open those wounds right when they've barely healed? Damn him, really. What gets into these people? So convinced their work is wonderful and yet you would think they were perfectly sane and capable of knowing that it was trash before they'd even come to the end of the first sentence! What thick mud seals their eyes? What blindness causes their brain paralysis? What dysfunction plagues their gray matter?

I tell him to come over. I stop working an hour before he gets there and try to relax. I go rake up some leaves in the garden and retie a rosebush. I top that off with some breathing exercises.

He comes inside. I tell him. For a second, I think he's going to explode, but actually he's in shock and he walks to the first place he finds to sit down. "Wow," he says.

"Richard, this is not about the quality of your work. Would you like some wine, maybe something stronger?"

"Then what is it if it's not the quality? I'd like to know."

"You know what it is. It's a business. They have particular tastes. There's nothing you or I can do about that. You just have to conform. You won't change anything. And you can be proud of that, in a way. Gin? Champagne?"

"You think this is a good time to drink champagne? Are we celebrating? I can tell you fought for me like crazy."

"It's not what they're looking for, Richard. I'm paid to know that. But maybe someone else will be interested. Try Gaumont. I think they're looking around for something new right now. You either adapt or you get swallowed up nowadays."

"Did you go to bat for me? Did you lift a finger?"

I don't answer. I hold out a gin and tonic. He stands up and, without a word, walks to the door. Vincent has the same goddamn stubborn character, it's unbelievable.

When the three of us were living together, they drove me crazy. I had to fix up the top floor so I could have some peace. On my dime, at Richard's insistence, even though he made significantly more than me at the time. He didn't want to put a penny toward my selfishness—or my whims, or my harebrained ideas, or my notions, depending.

Tempers flared, inevitably. I felt like I was cornered, hemmed in on both sides. It was like I had to pay for everything twice, like hearing an echo.

Now I'm speaking with Vincent and there's a storm outside. The sky suddenly darkened and the rain started to fall. It's cooler all of a sudden. A sweet odor of vegetable rot has filled the air. He tells me he got hired at McDonald's and he hopes he's going to get an advance when he signs his contract. He's in his car. He tells me that what I'm hearing are raindrops thundering down on the roof, but I don't hear a thing. He mixes in a thank you for the security deposit. He says it was cool of me to do that, that Josie says thank you as well.

When he finally shuts up for a second, I say, "You *hope* to get an advance on your salary? Vincent, what are you telling me?"

I build my first fire in the fireplace, nearing the end of November. I feel old and weary as I trudge inside with a few logs. Richard's reaction is almost enough to ruin my evening—that gesture of utter contempt, that scowl. Then I finally give in to the rain and Vincent's trouble getting together the money for his first month's rent. I start to cry.

Marty is there. The cat who stayed a few feet away as I was being raped. He sleeps on my bed. He eats with me. He follows me into the bathroom when I shower or shit, follows me when I go to bed with a man. He stops and looks at me. Seeing that I am neither screaming nor rolling around on the floor, he goes back to examining his rear paw, which he then licks a long moment. I look away.

Richard calls me the next day and says, "Did you have to work on that role of bitch you play so well, or does it just come naturally?" I had foreseen something of that nature. Hard feelings, bitterness, anger, insults. I don't think his work is worthless, but I know that no one will sink millions into this project and there's nothing I can do about that.

"No kidding! How can you say something like that? You stupid bitch. What do you know about it?"

His voice is trembling with contained anger. It couldn't be any other way, of course not. That's precisely why I'm so mad at him. For having set the wheels of this dread machinery in motion, so in one way or another it can once again tear us to shreds.

"Taking it out on me won't make your screenplay any better, Richard."

There's a second of silence and I swallow. Then I hear his forced, sneering laughter on the other end of the line. But I can just imagine the grimace he's really making as the pain deepens and spreads.

This is the first time in twenty years that I've clearly admitted that I'm not crazy about his work. I've always managed to dance around it, never dealing with it straight on, because I felt the whole building might tremble at the foundations. The subject could make it all unravel. And it still can, but at this point what can we lose that hasn't already been lost?

It's possible to love a man and not think he's the best screenwriter of all time. How I strove to make that point! Of what resource haven't I availed myself to bring him around to my view? But that was before I came to understand that I would never succeed, that he would never really accept any criticism coming from me. His very manhood was challenged if I didn't absolutely flip over his work, I could tell. And I cared about him enough that I didn't want to push it past the breaking point. I preserved our relationship with half-lies, half-truths, which I always wound up believing he could live with.

I really cared about a man for the first time in my life and I wanted to remain in his protection. It's as simple as that. My mother and I had had our share, and Richard was offering to look after us, to deliver us back to a normal life. Wasn't that worth something? And the more because I was attracted to him physically?

"Finally!" he says. "It took you long enough! But for once in your life you mustered a little courage! Nice going!"

"I got another message."

"What?"

"I got another message from the man who raped me."

"No, you've got to be kidding! You got *what*?"

"Are you deaf, Richard?"

I haven't seen my father in thirty years, haven't spoken to him. Yet he sends me a Polaroid, which my mother puts on the table. I lean over to look at it. It's hard for me to recognize him—the quality of the Polaroid isn't very good. I sit up straight and shrug. My mother watches me, hoping I'll make some comment. But I have none.

"Look how thin he is," she says. "I didn't lie to you about that."

"Let them force-feed him. Let them do their job."

We're at an outdoor café by the Seine. Last night's rain has hastened the falling of the leaves, and there are dark, seemingly empty nests clinging to the bare branches of the chestnut trees. Still, it's a nice day. I said I would see her at lunchtime even though I'm overloaded at work and I'm supposed to meet Anna at a screening on the other side of town. I ordered a *salade de gésiers* and my mother got the *andouillette de Troyes*. Sparkling water for both of us. "You're wasting your time, Mom. I will not go see him." The tip of my nose is cold. It's nice out, but the cool air has reached us.

"He's old now. You're his daughter."

"That doesn't mean anything to me. I'm his daughter. That no longer has any meaning."

"He would hold your hand for one minute and it would be done. You wouldn't even have to talk to him. He's wasting away daily now, you know?"

"Don't waste your breath. Eat."

I just don't understand why all of a sudden she has to cushion the end of this man's life. All those families in tears, all those angry families...has she forgotten them? And what about everything we went through for years because of him, because of what he did? Has she just wiped it from her brain?

"I finally learned forgiveness, Michèle."

"Is that right? Yes, I've heard of it. It's supposed to be nice. Are you happy with it? I'm so jealous of your shitty memory, you know? Shitty is the word. Really, really *shitty*."

When I meet Anna, I'm still furious. "We went through hell because of him, you know that. And all by herself she decides it's time to wipe out the past, just like that, as if with a magic wand. You have got to be kidding. Don't you think the old lady is going crazy?" Anna hands me a box of Chiclets. I take one. Chewing makes me feel better. Deep down, I would like to have her put in a cell. With him, if that's what she really wants. Bye-bye, Mom. This is where we part. I would love that. I'm ashamed to have those thoughts, but I would love it.

That dissolute life she leads—a sharp contrast to this Good Samaritan role she's playing with my father—is fairly annoying to me. She had better not push it. She's wrong to think she can nudge me into this last meeting. She's got an exaggerated idea of her power.

My boyfriend at the time, with whom I was head over heels in love, spit in my face when my father got arrested. And I know of nothing else so heartbreaking.

Evening falls as I get home. Now I only get out of the car holding the can of pepper spray and an army-issue flashlight, the weight and size of which is supposed to provide a decisive edge over my attacker. At least that's what the gun store guy said as he smacked the thing against the palm of his hand. I quickly scan a part of the one hundred fifty or so feet between my garage and my front door. The neighbor across the road mimes a friendly hello, then silently asks if everything's all right. I answer with an energetic nod.

A dark-colored car is parked near my house, a little down the block, partially hidden by a mass of persistent leaves. This is the second night I've seen it. Yesterday I either didn't have the courage or I was putting it off. Tonight I'm ready. Before, when it was parking, it was toward evening and I was standing at the window, rinsing rice. I straightened up.

There's no longer enough daylight to make out anything at all inside the car. I can't even really identify it now, with only a pale quarter-moon reddening a thin veil of high clouds, but I know he's there, at the wheel, that his thoughts are about me, that they're struggling mightily to reach me.

I am calm. Concentrating and tense. I am not afraid. Several times, I've had occasion to note that fear falls away when there is no longer any turning back, and I am in that situation now. I am determined. I wait. Let him come to me.

I have set up in the darkness, waiting for him to come out. I am ready for him. Ready to spray him, to make him pay. It's hardly ten o'clock but there's no one outside around here in November, not after nightfall. The coast is clear for him.

Suddenly, I can't believe it, I see the glow of a cigarette lighter. "He's got to be kidding," I blurt out loud, truly stunned.

At eleven o'clock, he lights a third cigarette. I want to scream in rage, but I hold it in. I can't stand this anymore. Throwing caution to the wind, along with any safety considerations, I decide to go to him since he's not coming to me. Squatting on my heels, I pull the door open a crack. I bite my lip and slip outside. I walk around the house so I can sneak up from behind. My breath is short, my legs wobbly, my jaw set tight. I've got my flashlight and my spray can as weapons, as well as my irrepressible will to get this over with.

A slight burning sensation is now my only souvenir of him, that and a few fading bruises. But it's no longer about what I feel physically. Like I said, I have had some experiences that I consider worse from the standpoint of penetration, strictly speaking. What's important is how I feel *in my head*. What's important is what he took from me *by force* and what at this instant I wield in my arm.

I have to use the element of surprise, just as he did. I was still in a state of shock when he pinned me to the ground. My heart hadn't even started beating again when he tore my underpants. I hadn't even figured out what was happening when he forced his way into me and took me.

I catch my breath. I gather my strength. I think about turning back, twisting my mouth up in silence, then my arm and the army flashlight form a semicircle and the passenger side window is blown apart.

I hear someone cry out but I'm already spraying the inside of the car, reaching through the shattered window. And really, so close to orgasm for one second, as I empty that can toward the shape now convulsing on the seat. I don't recognize poor Richard right away. He seems like he's on the verge of blacking out, but he manages to get the passenger door open and falls onto the pavement, moaning.

I've forgotten that Richard is also that man, worried about my safety despite our harsh exchanges. And I feel sorry about hurting his feelings with respect to his work, even if it was necessary. His eyes look terrible—red, swollen, bloodshot. I take him home because there's no way he can drive.

There's a woman in his life. This is when I find out. The car with the window I smashed belongs to her.

Not that I'm jealous. Richard and I have been separated for almost three years and I quickly put a few women in his path, to make the ordeal of divorce as painless as possible. I'm not jealous, but I'm not indifferent either. There are a lot of women in this business. They're drawn to the scene. And there were always a few who figured that a screenwriter with a couple of successes under his belt, who knew a lot of people, who wasn't half bad physically, might be worthy of a closer look. I didn't want them to be too intelligent either, or capable of devouring a man to the bone, or plotting and scheming. I was leery of the ones with big breasts, but also the ones who had read Sherwood Anderson or Virginia Woolf and would've chewed him up and spit him out.

Hélène Zacharian. I fill out an accident report in this woman's name. "She's *a* girlfriend," he tells me, "not *my* girlfriend."

"I wasn't asking."

I sign the accident report and put it in the glove compartment while he watches me with his irritated, tearful eyes. I take pity on him, I smile. I come up for a few minutes and he calls me a cab. Meanwhile, he makes some cold compresses out of Kleenex. I take a quick glance around and, although there is no item of clothing, no object that would reveal a woman's presence, I can feel a woman lives here. Or at least spends significant time here. I would even go farther. She was here only a few hours ago.

I learn more from Vincent, who doesn't seem to mind telling me about his father's new companion. He exaggerates his surprise. I didn't know? How is that even possible? Only five minutes ago, he had been wearing a yellow shirt, dark blue pants, and a red cap with a McDonald's logo screwed down tight on his head. I watched him from the sidewalk, cleaning the tables, stacking the trays, as if wandering around in the rubble. I had to look away. A cool wind comes whipping down the avenue like an invisible flame.

I've just come from a meeting with a writer who agreed to write a screenplay based on his novel, after making a quick calculation. An interesting guy that I've decided to keep an eye on.

To hear Vincent tell it, they've been together for a few

weeks and she's much younger than he is. "I don't understand why he never told you about this."

It's both strange and very clear to me—and to him, of course.

There are two floors between us. Hélène Zacharian works on the thirty-second floor, at Hexagone. AV Productions is on thirty. Vincent thinks we could have a meal or two together, might as well, but that doesn't make me laugh.

How's Josie? She's fine. She's enormous. She's gained sixty-five pounds, maybe more. She can hardly move anymore, she just lies around in front of the TV. I touch his arm and ask him if he's really sure about this. He gives me a look of disdain and pushes my hand away, like it was something hideous. Ungrateful child that I carried inside me, that I made myself from scratch, that I plucked from nothingness!

I'm a little peeved at being kept at bay, especially since I wasn't expecting it. I'm a little troubled by the idea that Richard might start over. Oh, now I'm demoralized for the rest of the day. I make an attempt with Anna but turn down her invitation when she tells me that Robert is back. That sick exercise he and I indulge in regularly in front of her, not giving ourselves away—an exercise that he says "adds spice" to our relationship—is now absolute torture for me.

Night comes and I try to work for a while, or watch a movie, but I give up. I can't concentrate. I go outside. I smoke a cigarette but stay near the door, carrying my Guardian Angel. It's December and it's no longer chilly, but for the first time really cold. Night is black as ink, the sky is clear, the crescent moon as thin as steel wire, and dull. It's late. The silence and dark around me feel threatening. But that threat is alluring, keeps me up, electrifies me to the core. Actually, I think I'm crazy. I think I want him to be there, lurking in the shadows. Want him to leap out at me and fight, so I can measure myself against him, with all my strength, kicking, punching, biting, grabbing his hair, tying him up naked next to my window. Lord, how could I have such horrifying thoughts?

If I were a normal woman, I'd stop paying my mother's rent and have her move into the house with me. My accountant, who is an unpleasant-looking man with shifty eyes but who has always given me good advice, says I should think carefully about the future, and he's the one who gives me the idea about Irène's rent. After thinking it over, that's what I would probably do if I were a normal woman, who thought logically, but logic has nothing to do with this. I simply do not have the energy I would need to live with her—much less the patience, the desire, or the will. I shake my head. I realize that nothing will ever be easy again, that the best years are behind us, that we have very definitely left our glory days behind. Now it's time to seek security, reduce expenses, save, and so on. But sometimes it's better to die than to live half a life, in sort of a state of permanent frenzy and madness. I tell him I'll think about it.

I had a bad night, mulling over the day's events, thinking about the fact that Richard met a woman, about Robert's return, about the absurdity of the couple Vincent and Josie have formed, about the nauseating relationship

I have with my mother, and those horrible thoughts that go through my mind when I think of my attacker. What a moribund, ghastly night, one that a handful of pills could do nothing to change. All this to say that I would have preferred to begin my day with something other than a visit from my accountant, telling me that times are hard, Europe is still on shaky ground, and the future looks bleak. But that's not all. No sooner do I pop an aspirin than Robert slips into my office and closes the door behind him, carefully, a finger on his lips. "Excuse me, Robert, but…" I was going to explain that I have a lot of work to do and that this isn't a good time, but in a flash he's all over me, going for my lips. I have said that he's a good enough lover, but I must admit that I'm not a fan of those wet kisses, his ramming his tongue into my mouth with all the delicacy of an ill-tempered teenager. When I do manage to separate our mouths, he opens his fly and tells me I can touch it. "In that case, stand over the trash can," I say.

Toward noon, after a mind-numbing meeting with the head of programming at a cable channel—who only last month was still a midlevel exec at L'Oréal and who thinks that *Mad Men* is a documentary about a psychiatric hospital—I decide it's time to go snoop around Hexagone.

Hélène Zacharian and I do indeed work in the same office building, only two floors apart, and she is a ravishing brunette with bright eyes who works at reception. I think I've seen her in the elevator a couple of times. I think I should be worried. "I'm Richard's ex," I tell her, sticking my hand out across the frosted glass countertop, a big smile on my face, trying to seem as cheerful as I possibly can.

"Oh, nice to meet you. This is so great," she answers, shaking my hand warmly.

"We should meet one of these days," I say. "At least Richard won't have to introduce us now."

"Right, of course. Whenever you want."

"Well, let's say next week sometime. I'll work it out with Richard, don't worry about a thing."

I take the stairs back down because I don't want to wait for the elevator while she watches. My heels click nervously on the concrete steps of the emergency staircase as I beat my hasty retreat.

Let's be truthful: She's about fifteen years younger than me and she's every bit as fine as I feared.

For as long as my mother refused to move, we were subjected to every last vexation, every torment in the world. I was already twenty—my father had been in solitary confinement for five years, having been labeled "Monster of the Aquitaine" for slaughtering seventy children in a seaside resort day camp—when I met Richard. He is the only one other than Irène who really knew me young, but he is also the one who changed my life, who, any way you slice it, saved my mother and me. And I'm suddenly afraid to lose all of that.

This is the first time in my life that I feel like I could lose Richard, and that takes its toll. Anna holds me to her shoulder for a moment, kisses my forehead, orders us each a croque monsieur, a salad with Abruzzo oil, and bottled water.

Later we go to the movies, then she sees me home, and all of a sudden she wants to have a last smoke outside my door before she goes. We turn up our collars, smoke with our gloves on. I tell her she kept this evening from veering morose. She answers, "Good, you owe me one." I look up at the sky, all lit up with stars tonight. "I was raped, Anna. It happened almost two weeks ago."

Without looking away from the firmament, I wait for her reaction, but it doesn't come. Maybe she's dead or all of a sudden she's gone deaf or she isn't listening. "Did you hear me?" I feel her hand closing around my arm. Then she blanches, turns to me. Petrified. Holds me close. Both of us stock-still. Deathly silent. Profoundly stupid. I can feel her breath on my neck.

We go inside. She tosses her coat on the couch. I light a fire. We stare at one another once again. Then she catches her breath and doesn't ask me how I feel. She knows. Of course. She tells me I shouldn't have waited so long to tell her and I try to explain what a state of uncertainty I had found myself in, and naturally I had tried to bury the whole thing at first. "Oh, listen," I say, "it wasn't that simple. I wasn't really in pain. It wasn't like it was Patrick Bateman, all right? I was perfectly capable of closing my eyes, never mentioning it to anyone. It was the easiest way. I didn't know what to do, you know?"

"Hiding something like that from me. Christ."

"Besides Richard, you're the first person I've told."

"You tell Richard about it and you don't tell me. Come on, explain that one!"

I walk over and sit down next to her and we watch the fire take, the flames leaping up toward the purring chimney. With each passing second, I am sorrier that I let Robert come on to me and that I hadn't ended the affair. I think what a price there would be to pay if she ever found out, and I tremble by her side. I think what a coward I've been, what an absolutely horrible example I've set. And I shiver all over until she rubs my back and says again and again, everything's all right, there, there, as if I were about to break down and sob.

Anna told me that I had screamed without stopping from the moment they admitted me in the wee hours until late that evening when I finally gave birth—freed my body in one last excruciating torment of the relentless creature that had resided within it and persecuted it by twisting my bladder, for example, night and day, or else starving me or depriving me of cigarettes.

She was in the next room and she had just lost her child, and my screaming would have driven her mad, she told me, if she hadn't wound up getting up and coming to keep me company. I had spaced out my moaning and we spent a few hours together and later she told me that the trauma she went through would be a tiny bit easier to bear because of the child I would bring into the world, compensation for hers.

This morning, Josie found blood in her underwear and they rushed to the hospital, where I joined them with coffee and croissants I bought at the cafeteria. She appreciates me coming and, if I'm going to keep an eye on a situation that Vincent doesn't seem to be in control of at all, I don't want her to see me as her enemy.

"If it's now, she's early," Vincent explains.

"Vincent," says Josie, "your mother can count."

It doesn't take much to get the measure of a couple's state of affairs. One remark, sometimes one glance, one silence, and it's all very clear. With that, a nurse comes to take Josie away and Vincent tells me he's decided to recognize the child. And I immediately think, *Why give birth to such idiots?* I had sworn to myself that I would no longer weigh in about this life they were starting together, but I just can't help myself now.

"Do you ever think? Do you know what you're committing to? It's a prison sentence, Vincent. You're walking into prison. Don't look away, my son, look at the reality. Do you hear me? It's a cage. Those are chains. A prison." I give up, wave him off, before he even opens his mouth to answer. He has already looked daggers at me, gone pale. A vein has pulsated on his forehead. I am the worst thing that ever happened to him.

Josie comes back on a gurney and, looking grave, tells us she is going to give birth within an hour. I meet Vincent's eyes for a second before he runs to Josie, and the look in those eyes is one of a scared child. And I in no way want to reassure him. I'm convinced they won't last long. Living in this city requires having at least a little money, which they obviously don't have, so it won't take long. The only thing is, the life they get back to will be a little bit more complicated than it had been to start with, a little harder to disentangle, but you can't go back, what's done is done.

I wouldn't want to be in Josie's shoes. If I think about the ordeal she's about to go through, I might get sick. When some women tell me that the experience of giving birth was like having an orgasm, I laugh right in their faces. I have rarely heard such gibberish. It's like listening to some throwback to another era, brains fried by sunshine and acid flashbacks. A thousand deaths. That's what I went through to have Vincent. A thousand deaths, and not a thousand delights. Let's be serious. Let's not be afraid to tell the truth.

It's a beautiful day, cold and bright. The air smells good. A good day to go for a walk around town, and I keep to the busy streets. I send Vincent a message to ask if he needs anything, but his terse reply means he hasn't softened.

I try to call him several times that afternoon but he doesn't answer. Then I have a long session at work with two writers on a series who experience every cut I request, every correction, every drop of red ink as a personal assault, a blow below the belt, an affront to their genius. One of them even winds up pounding his fist on the desk and walking out into the hallway and slamming the door. When he comes back, he seems to have calmed down and we continue to the next problem, which doesn't take too long to emerge.

I only let them go at sundown and they are in a horrible mood. I can't get over their monstrous egos, how sure they are of their own value, considering they are most often mediocre, almost never good. We part ways in the parking lot, murmuring vague goodbyes, and one of them—a blond guy about thirty with sharp, angular features and stringy hair—wears a smile strange enough to make me think that there, he could be a guy like that, someone I've treated poorly, whose work I disparaged, some guy whose intelligence, superiority, quality I have questioned. Especially coming from a woman. Night has fallen. I wouldn't want to be alone with him in the middle of a field.

Vincent finally calls me from a phone booth—his minutes all gone—when I'm passing the Louvre in heavy traffic. The Place de la Concorde is an ocean of red lights with wavy interior currents, slow and mysterious.

"Jesus, Mom! It's a boy!" He screams into my ear, delirious with excitement.

"Fine, Vincent. But it's not *your* boy. Don't lose sight of that."

"I'm incredibly happy, you know? Incredibly happy." He's breathing hard, like he was jumping rope.

"Did you hear me, Vincent?"

"What? No, what did you say?"

"I said he's not really yours, Vincent. That's all I'm saying. So how much does he weigh?"

An icy silence on the other end of the line. "Well, whose is he if he's not mine?" he asks suddenly, with a very marked change of tone. I can feel the storm coming, no mistake about it, but nothing can be done. "Is he yours?" he asks in a hiss. "Whose is he? The pope's?"

"He's his father's, I guess. And you're not his father, Vincent."

I know what he's doing. He's banging the receiver against a wall or something else. A gesture of pure rage. This is not the first time he's dabbled in the art. He has confided to me that it's not exactly the telephone he wants to smash in such moments. "Vincent," I told him, "I can't wait for the day when you lift a hand to me." Then we drank to one another, because we were in a good mood that night and we managed to have a sense of humor about ourselves and keep it simple. I've hidden nothing from this boy about the hell into which his birth once threw me, but I have never told him what mind-boggling love I felt for him — and I still love him, I guess. Vincent is my son, though with time everything warms over. I wasn't particularly thrilled about having to nurse him. But then what happiness he gave me, what a sense of fulfillment he provided — such a new and unexpected sensation — what never-ending joy there was in being a mother. That is, up until the first girls appeared on the scene.

It was conceiving this child that saved me from the psychological shipwreck my father had dragged me into. Vincent brought me back to life, such a marvel, so different from the inconsequential lout who is part of my life now, the one who's about to become the father of a child who isn't his, after marrying the mother. This kind of thing works out well maybe one time in a thousand. And who is going to tell him that, if not me?

Certainly not Richard, who seems to have other priorities right now. I admit I'm not quite as indifferent as I should be with regard to this new life he's building for himself without even bothering to let me know. Oh, I know he's not obliged to tell me anything, but we lived together for twenty years and I slept with him for twenty years, I ate across the table from him, we shared a bathroom, a car, computers, anyway...So I don't know, I don't know if he owes me anything at all, I don't know if I deserve to be kept up to speed about his plans, I don't know if I'm anything but a piece of dog shit for him, well, sometimes I wonder.

So certainly not him, not the guy who always came down on the side of his son as our relationship went south and whose movie projects were invariably put on hold.

Despite this, I call him to talk about it and he tells me, "I'm at the hospital." My blood courses through my veins and I nearly ram into the car in front of me, but he adds, "I stepped out for a smoke. Vincent doesn't want to talk to you."

I feel I should be there, not here. Richard's presence on the scene makes me feel guilty. "I want to be sure we're on the same page here," I say. "I'd like you to use this opportunity to talk to him, make him realize he shouldn't be rushing into things, making lifelong commitments in a hasty manner. Hello. Can you hear me?"

"I don't think there is any right way to make lifelong commitments."

"Well, there's a wrong way, believe me. He doesn't know anything. He's still a little boy, can't you see that? I'm not saying she's wicked, I'm not criticizing his choice, but it's just a little *too rushed*. Isn't it? Isn't that obvious to you? Can't you see what he's diving into headlong? I'm wondering if you've actually taken the time to really look at them, if you still have time for that. I'm sorry, Richard, but I do honestly wonder."

"Settle down."

"Actually, I'm very unsettled. I'm not sure you're up to the task here. But okay, look. I'm going to have dinner at my place as soon as Josie gets out of the hospital. The whole family together. Anna and Robert will be there, and so will my mother. I've invited your girlfriend as well. I thought she was lovely, by the way. You could do the shopping, what do you say? You could introduce us to your new flame."

I could've sworn I heard him gnashing his teeth and I could just picture his eyes squint and his shoulders drop. "I'm not going to make a big deal," I say, "but I wish I could have heard it first from you." I hang up before he does. I'm not saying I have the sweetest nature, and I can act like a real bitch, that's for sure, but seriously he deserved that. He hurt me. I finally get out of the Place de la Concorde and I drive over the bridge of the same name, my teeth clenched, my eyes misting over. I just realized that I actually no longer have a husband, a son, or a father. I drive along the river, glance at the houseboats, those monstrous *bateaux-mouches* floating restaurants, the homeless people camping on the banks. I draw no conclusions, I'm just taking stock. I'm all alone and floating, and it's like I'm caught up short, disconcerted.

When I get home, I literally cross paths with my neighbor from across the road, Patrick What's-His-Name. He appears in my headlights, staggering across the narrow strip of pavement, holding his head. He comes straight toward me as I get out of the car. "Get inside, quick! There's a prowler!"

"There's a what?"

"Get inside, Michèle. Don't stay out here. That asshole practically knocked me out. Go inside, lock the doors. I'm going to take a look around."

"I could lend you my flashlight if you want. Are you all right? You're not injured, are you?"

"No, go ahead, don't worry. I'll return it tomorrow. Go.

He better make sure I don't get my hands on him. A word of friendly advice."

Those words taste like blood. There's steam coming from his nostrils in the even colder night air. I'm not a famous person, my name is right there on my mailbox for all to see, but I'm still surprised he called me by my first name, like it was the most natural thing in the world, when in reality we have never exchanged more than three words and a few nods hello ever since they moved in last spring. Hello. How are you? I don't know what to think about it. I turn my alarm off and invite him in.

"My wife is still shaking," he tells me. We go into the kitchen, I give him the flashlight. I pour him a glass of water. I don't even really know who this guy is. He wants me to write down his phone number, tells me to call him any time of day or night if there's trouble. He tells me that's what neighbors are for. Then he ventures out into the night, on the heels of his assailant.

If you ask me, there's a good chance it's the same man. And, in a way, I sort of regret that Patrick ran him off. Not that I have a precise plan or desire, not that there's anything whatsoever to justify this morbid attraction he works on me. But just the idea that he's really watching me, that the veil might have been lifted tonight, that we could have settled the score immediately—whatever price I might pay—makes Patrick's stepping in and wasting the chance a bitter pill to swallow.

But Patrick is a good guy, a bank executive, still surprised at the size of the pile he's made for himself, at how easy it had been to become a homeowner prior to the Great

Crisis of 2007, which brought us where we are and which never seems to be over. He brings my flashlight back in the early morning, asks how well I slept after the incidents of the previous night.

"Let's try not to make high drama out of this, Patrick. It isn't worth it."

"The police told me they would beef up patrols."

"Great. You know, I don't want to have to drive you to the hospital with a knife in your back or your skull cracked open with a log. So show me you can be a little more careful than you were last night. Please, don't go overboard. You're young. Don't wind up on a stretcher or God knows what."

I think he's the type to play squash with a branch manager because he looks like he's in good shape. We had a big dog when I was a child, and the problem we had was that we couldn't tire him out. My father took him on long walks after he got home from work but it wasn't enough, and all night long we could hear the animal pacing around the kitchen, inexhaustible. Finally, my father put him down. That's what this Patrick does to me; he's a ball of energy, but it's a vain, useless kind of energy. When he and his wife came over to introduce themselves, right after they moved in, I didn't really notice. I made some joke about having a banker as a next-door neighbor in times like these, that it was like knowing a farmer during a period of famine, and it took him a while to react. He had a weak handshake and, honestly, I didn't see the action hero, the type A personality in him. The change is surprising. I wouldn't be surprised to learn he takes DHEA or some kind of amphetamine, but they say you need nerves of steel to work in finance, that those little darlings are under horrible pressure according to the markets. "But thank you, Patrick," I say, tugging the collar of my bathrobe snugly to my throat, because it's a nice day but the sun provides practically no heat and cold air is whistling through the trees and the bushes. "I'm a grandmother," I add, as he smiles goodbye.

Don't ask me why I say this, or exactly what it means. But I certainly don't expect it will win me a compliment. "Oh, congratulations," he answers, looking me straight in the eyes.

I spend the day at home, my screenplays all around me, allowing myself only a walk in the neighboring wood, bundled up, a woolen hat on my head, enjoying the bright light, the biting cold, the carpet of autumnal leaves, the squawk of birds, and the tranquil, subtle calm of a fall afternoon. After miles of notes and suggestions, passages to be reworked, developed, clarified, thrown out, underlined in red, once, twice, three times, ad nauseam, and never finding anything truly satisfying. There is still some misty undergrowth, certain clumps of bushes remain in darkness, but I never get off the paths. There is a map of the wood at the top of the hill where some retired seniors are gathered, with their exercise clothes on—spandex tights and bright yellow headbands, futuristic sneakers, phones strapped to their arms, earbuds, red cheeks, and drippy noses. I can see the roof of the house below, through half-bare branches, the home of my closest neighbors, Patrick and his wife, the gate outside the Audret family house, all lit up for the holidays. To the left, a small set of six condos. Then the rest gets lost in the trees, with the exception of the local area minimart, which can be picked out because of the brick-colored pavement in the parking lot and the banners whipping proudly in the wind.

I smoke a cigarette while the aging athletes exchange energy bars and vitamin drinks.

I'm not sure I want to get that old, but that, too, could change. I can't say that Patrick is exactly my kind of man either, but compared to Robert, whose touch no longer thrills me in the least, my young banker does awaken some fuzzy feelings in me. And that is fairly huge because it's the first sign of a sexual awakening since the rape, and thank heavens. I'll once again be able to hold a man in my arms. I was so afraid, I was so terribly afraid that something in me just snapped and that all of that was behind me. I'm not so demoralized now. I go home. I masturbate while thinking of him, I bite my lips, the machine still works. I am practically in tears I'm so happy, so grateful. I wipe my fingers, keep my eyes closed for a whole minute.

I'm upstairs, in my bedroom, when he gets home. I'm in the dark. I even turned off the screen of my iPad when he got out of his car. I'm watching him through binoculars. He's much better looking than he was in my mind when we only waved and said hello like neighbors. He's much more alert, much more vigorous. That forced smile I had when he made that first impression on me! I follow him with my eyes. I know this is just because it's easily available and that I'd be better off going into town where I would get a wider menu. Patrick is the most common sort of man at parties—the pleasant and artificial sort, narcissistic and noncommittal, in a Ralph Lauren polo shirt. It probably wouldn't be hard to do better than that, but I don't feel like it. I think there are times when making the easy choice is the better part of wisdom.

I take pleasure in spying on a man from the darkness of my bedroom. I feel a kind of childlike excitement. I hide halfway behind the curtain while he opens his door and glances one more time behind, toward *me*, and even though he can't see me, I hold my breath. This is new, or rather, very old—and it's fun, it's nice. When he goes inside, I go up to the attic for a better view of the windows in his house. From downstairs they're hidden by the branches Richard didn't trim on purpose, to protect our privacy when that was still important to him. I can see him moving behind the lighted windows, little illuminations floating in the night—Patrick hanging up his coat, Patrick crossing his living room, Patrick kissing his wife, Patrick in his bathroom, Patrick leaning over his sink...and then suddenly my phone rings.

"What are you doing?" asks Richard.

"Nothing. I'm reading. What do you want?"

"I want to explain why I didn't tell you."

"Look, I don't care."

"I didn't tell you about it because I'm just not fucking sure about anything."

"You're never sure about anything, ever notice that?"

"Come on, why would I hide it from you if there was anything to it? How would I benefit?"

"Richard, I'm busy."

"You're reading. You call that busy? Isn't that a little much? Anyway, I want to know if you're setting me up."

"What?"

"I want to know if you're setting me up."

"And you think I would just tell you? You think I would do that?"

"Still, I don't see what would justify it. I don't get how I'm guilty here. I've played by our rules. We owe each other the truth. I totally agree. And the truth is, there is nothing really brewing. I'm sort of seeing the girl, fine. But I didn't tell you about it because, in my estimation, there is nothing to talk about."

"What makes you think I'm setting you up for something?"

"That fucking invitation! Inviting her to fucking dinner!"

"Nice. You manage to work 'fucking' into every sentence. Really very nice."

"It feels like a trap. It feels like one of your world-famous traps."

"You're losing it here, honey. I've got better things to worry about, you know. Don't get paranoid. And by the way, is there anything she won't eat? Any allergies at all? Marty is shedding like crazy."

Many married women are great mistresses and I think he is *taking risks* with a single woman. I remind him that we agreed *not to take risks*, precisely in order to avoid this kind of problem, and I ask him if this is what he sees as *not taking risks*, splashing around in those waters with single women of childbearing age. Or is he just putting me on?

When I hang up I find myself alone in my attic, tossed among dusty and useless things, while Patrick suddenly disappears into the darkness of his bedroom just when his wife joins him in her nightgown.

There is nothing much to fear from women who wear nightgowns. Generally, their husbands are there for the taking.

Anna comes by to pick up the three screenplays I've chosen and I warn her that there isn't much to get excited about. "I don't know how you do it," she says. "In your shoes I'd already have an attack dog." She stays for dinner. She has stopped on the way at Chez Flo's and decides she would rather share the meal with me than with Robert, who has been so on edge since he got back.

I know he's on edge, I get his messages, I can see he's calling me. I try not to think about it because I'm not at all crazy about what could happen if he took it the wrong way. If he took my lack of interest in him the wrong way, the distance between us steadily and irreversibly growing. And if he found out that I've been fantasizing about my neighbor across the street, that merely thinking about him makes me feel sexually vulnerable, something could happen. Something I don't want to think about, don't want to imagine. Something approaching chaos could happen.

First and foremost, I think my friendship with Anna would split apart and disappear into thin air. I have practically no memory of my relationships before the day my father walked out of the house armed to the teeth. I never saw anyone again in any case. And Anna rushed into this unoccupied space and I have only her. Other than the members of my family I have only her. I don't want to test it.

There's no reckless gambler in me when it comes to her. I don't want to test anything at all.

Knowing the scope of her feelings for her husband, a betrayal in love would have little to do with what would break the bond between us, but a betrayal in friendship would, yes, no question. She would never forgive me for doing that, behind her back—no more than I would have forgiven her myself—and yet I want to tell her just how much I feel like I *slid* into the relationship with her husband, got dragged into it, went down an irresistible mental incline that made me numb. I want to tell her just how pathetic our battles are, but I think she already knows.

Robert was the easy choice, too. Boredom, proximity, security. But there is no one here who could make that sad assessment and jump to hasty conclusions. My job left me no more time than it does now, and finding a relationship is not simple when you leave the office in the dead of night and you're bringing work home and you have no appetite. Robert could adapt to my schedule and the good news was he could get his hands on Christian Louboutins for half price and he was on the road for long periods of time. It's almost laughable. The other good news is that over twenty-five years Anna and I had other things to think about besides our love lives, and we built a solid company, put together a catalog we could be proud of, and even sold a few ideas to the Americans. AV Productions. She was already talking about it when we were in the hospital, chewed my ear for hours. She was resolute and, when I got home, I told Richard we could now look for an apartment with an extra bedroom for our kid because I had found a job.

"Huh? What job?"

"Anna and I are going to produce a movie."

"Produce a movie? Oh, fine. What a great fucking idea."

He's crying at our door now and blames me for not using my pull to help him, but being completely without a sense of humor he doesn't get the irony and he goes on thinking that for some dark and inexplicable reason I am blocking his way to the top, ever since he got it into his head to write screenplays. I did pay for his writing classes with the best people out there, the Vince Gilligans and the Matthew Weiners, guys who won WGA prizes, but they couldn't convey the gift they have, never being on the outside but on the inside, being generous, the gift they have in any case to elevate entertainment to the level of fine art. I think it will probably take a generation or two before someone actually can play in the same league with those guys and not get laughed out of the room. Perhaps less; there are some emerging names locally, especially among the writers. Anyway, what's the difference? Those classes cost a fortune, a veritable fortune, and Richard hasn't yet shown he got anything out of them, even though he says he did.

I go smoke a cigarette outside after Anna leaves. I don't stray. I keep leaning against the wall. I'm just showing that I'm not frightened out of my wits, that I'm not hiding under my bed. Anna offered to let me sleep at her place for as long as I liked, but it wasn't because I would be living under the same roof as Robert that I declined the invitation—though that idea was enough to make my hair stand on end and frown, horrified. No, I don't know what exactly

I'm looking for. It's cold, the days are getting shorter. I'm not reading any good screenplays. I've been raped. I don't talk about my relationships with my husband and my son, I don't even hint at anything about my parents. The worst part is it's time to start thinking about presents.

Fine, there wasn't much time to tidy up and they were probably very rushed trying to finish painting as they had planned, but it's a total shambles and it doesn't smell right—a whiff of shit and sour milk. Never mind. I have stuffed all my resentment, every hurtful remark, each negative thought into the bottom of a big black bag that I tied up tight and left on the doorstep of their new apartment.

"Fabulous!" I say as I sit down at the kitchen table with Josie, who is wearing baggy sweats, baby at her breast. Unlike many mothers, I hate kissing the soft, crimson cheeks of a newborn, but I say, "He's so gorgeous. Can I kiss him?"

Vincent said something about sixty-five pounds, but I think it's more like a hundred. She's enormous, she doesn't look like she just gave birth. She hands me the child, saying that now he has the same name as I do. "Oh, that little rascal," I say, holding the infant high over my head. Then I give him another little peck and hand him back.

"Now let's get down to brass tacks," I say. "What would you like for Christmas?"

They look at one another, puffing out their cheeks.

I help them out: "Kids, how would you feel about a good washing machine? With a newborn, that would be just the thing. Don't you agree?" They stare back at me like I'm trying to sell them a bill of goods.

"A vacuum cleaner? A sewing machine? A Kenwood food processor? An oven? A dishwasher? A fabric steamer? A refrigerator?"

"I think I'd rather have a good flat-screen and lots of pay channels," says Josie.

I nod. "Yeah, but I'd advise you to go with the most important thing first—"

"That's what I'm doing," she says, cutting me off. "Next is the stereo and after that the DVR."

I smile because, after killing the dog, the television was what my father went for, throwing ours out the window, and our troubles started right at that moment, because the neighbors weren't happy having such a bad-tempered fellow in their midst, someone so estranged from their values, who spoke of holing up in Brittany as soon as unrest broke out in the streets of the capital, and who made the sign of the cross on the foreheads of children he passed on the stairs, and who asked him?

I call Richard to make sure he hasn't forgotten to do the shopping for the next day, and he immediately picks up our previous conversation. "Listen," I say, "save your breath. Marry her if you want to, I couldn't care less."

"Are you fucking tripping or what?"

"Or don't marry her, I couldn't care less."

"Do not make a scene tomorrow. Don't do something we'll all regret. Let's not start fighting over her, all right?"

"I'm not fighting with you, Richard. I didn't call you to listen to you whining over the phone. Do whatever you want. Don't feel you have to tell me anything at all. You're free to do as you please. I don't see why I have to keep telling you that. I invited the girl to make you happy. Is that clear? Can we talk about something else now? Are you done with this?"

"You can't reject my work and at the same time keep me from having my own life. That's a lot for me to take at once."

"Just don't show up too late. I won't be able to do everything myself. Will your girlfriend help us?"

I let him get off the phone. His stubborn denial that he has a serious relationship with this Hélène Zacharian is now frankly ludicrous.

I spend part of the afternoon sorting through the countless screenplays cluttering up the bookshelves in my office and piling up on the floor in precarious dirty white towers. But Anna and I will not let anyone else do the reading and, whatever I may have implied, I still experience the same emotion, the same thrill each time I read a first page, with the thought that it might be something exceptional, or even relatively good.

Anna pokes her head in toward closing time and takes a quick glance around. She congratulates me on doing a chore she's going to have to do herself pretty soon. "I just spoke to Vincent," she goes on. "I swore I wouldn't say anything, but do you know about his debts?"

I am already sitting down, so all I can do is squeeze the armrests on my chair and lean forward. "What are you talking about, Anna? What debts?"

She doesn't really know. He isn't really saying. It's pretty vague. She gives him money. It's nothing at all that she gives him money—she's his godmother—she's thrilled she can be of use to him, she tells me as we ride the elevator down from thirty. "This is a total shock to me," I say.

He's only twenty-four. I didn't think you could have real debt at twenty-four. All of a sudden, I feel like he's much older than he is, struck by an affliction that normally doesn't occur before thirty, or not without some serious bad luck. How did he manage to get into debt? The word itself sounds to me like some shameful malady. Drugs? Girls? Gambling? Anna makes me promise I won't get unduly alarmed but just be vigilant. "Fine," I say, "but could you explain to me what that means exactly? Considering that he doesn't live with me and tells me off as often as he possibly can. What exactly do you mean by vigilant? Give me an idea of what I can do, in your opinion. Enlighten me. He tells you more than he tells me, Anna. I'm the last person he would confide in, you know that very well. I'm his mother. I'm the woman who tossed his father out of the house. I'm the most horrible thing in the world."

We walk together in the crisp air for a few minutes, silent, arms linked, then we go into a bar and order up some daiquiris. "I want to pay you back," I tell her. She says no. Not just out of her generous spirit but because she wants to keep up this special relationship they have, which she worked to achieve right from the beginning. I let her nurse him a couple of times when we were still in the hospital and they used that to establish a mysterious, exceptional bond, which can still be felt today, a direct bond, which of course doesn't depend on me in the least. I can still see her wiping away a tear and watching it land on Vincent's forehead while he suckled her shamelessly and I was young then and that image really got to me. I was glad that my son and I could ease her suffering, and I would do it all over again, but it annoys me a little that she knows things before I do, that she knows what's going on in the family before I'm even informed, that she works out certain problems instead of me.

"I consider him like my son," she says. "You know that. I helped him out, that's all. It's between him and me. It's done."

"You're his spiritual mother. You're not his bank."

She gets up to get us two more daiquiris.

"There is another possibility," she says when she gets back. "Meaning Josie."

She looks straight at me, her bright eyes locked on mine, burning right through me.

When she says "meaning Josie," she's implying Josie might be the source of Vincent's problems. "I helped him out the first time just after they met. I'm not sure that's a coincidence. That's what I'm getting at."

I use a straw to drink without breaking eye contact. Then I deliberately let her hear the horrible noise of sucking at the bottom of the empty glass.

I'm not jealous of Vincent's girlfriends and I haven't been for a long time. In fact, I sort of pity the poor dears, having to deal with such a foul-tempered person—unless I have an exclusive on his bitterness and resentment. I can't rule that out. Anna says she's not jealous either and contends that the negative judgments she keeps making about the poor dears do not emanate from any preconceived notion. But she is always quick to denigrate them, or kick them, at every opportunity. "I don't call that being jealous," she says. "I help him to open his eyes, which isn't the same thing. Because when you get right down to it, he still doesn't have the slightest idea. He's still just a child." I'm not sure Vincent is still just a child. I would even say he stopped being one the day he refused to hold my hand on the way to school. But the fact that he's stupid enough to move in with a two-hundred-pound woman and hurriedly recognize her child, which is not his, is ample proof that he has the mentality of a slightly retarded teenager who eschews any reasonable attitude.

"I think Josie is at the root of what's wrong," she says. "I'm not jumping to conclusions, you know? I don't want to look like I'm defending him no matter what, but I'll tell you one thing, Vincent did not have this kind of problem before he met her. You draw your own conclusions, Michèle. You decide if it's my imagination."

"I don't know. I'm listening. I'm thinking."

"First of all, tell me. Do we know who the father is? You don't know? That's pretty incredible, isn't it? Anything is possible. Something really horrible, perhaps."

She reads too many screenplays, that's for sure. That is why she hunts down every possible avenue, all the ramifications. But I still have the feeling Anna is right, and I'm relieved at the thought that Vincent is not on the front line of this. This is much better. I was already imagining that he owed money to a bunch of Hells Angels or the senior executives of an investment bank.

The first thing I notice when I get home is the light on in my bedroom window. The curtain is floating softly in the breeze. I stay in the car for a moment, inspecting the area, bathed in pools of public lighting. But there is nothing stirring. There is no light on at the neighbors'. Everything is absolutely quiet and calm. And so am I, surprisingly, although "absolutely" is overstating it just a little considering that I'm gripping my can of pepper spray so tightly in my fingers that I can feel pain shooting up into my shoulder.

I unlock my front gate, wait a few seconds before I open it. Then I put one foot forward and, seeing that nothing special happens, the other foot as well. Adrenaline courses through me like lukewarm juice. In the time it takes to get to my front door, there is sweat on my brow and I'm short of breath.

I put my ear to the door. I hear nothing. I take out my key.

Inside, the alarm is activated. I turn it off. Nothing downstairs. I go upstairs—I know the sound of every step, which one groans, which one crackles. I make no noise at all.

The door to my bedroom is open to the dark hallway. I go inside, my heart pounding. The bed is all undone, the covers thrown on the ground. My dresser is open, my panties strewn around. On the bedside table, the screen on my cell phone is lit up. I move toward it.

And that's when I discover the disgusting, slimy, stinky stain on the sheets, with which someone obviously wiped himself—accompanied by the message, "Oh, sorry! I just couldn't wait!" kindly posted on the screen.

I look up and I am briefly lost in contemplation of the curtain dancing at the open window.

Richard gets there in the early afternoon, arms full. I myself got out early to buy the nuts and starters, the dessert and wine. I'm bringing in some wood for the fire when he beeps the horn.

I can see at a glance that he's going to be charming and helpful with me, and I think he has made the right decision, I think he knows me well. Because in fact it is a little hard to welcome the woman who's taking my son and the woman who's taking my husband at my table at the same time, to put it melodramatically, even though I am trying to be as broad-minded as possible. I know I'm going to have to relax, I'm going to have to find something to do with this stress that I woke up with early this morning, right when I opened my eyes, and that hasn't left me since. Bringing in the wood is one of the things that is supposed to calm me down, because it's so heavy. Richard got a good deal on some one-meter logs from the Landes region, which had been devastated by the hurricane, but moving them around is no picnic.

He carries in the groceries and immediately comes back outside to help me. It's a fine, cold day.

"I'll come by to see to the garden," he says, "soon as I get some time. I'll come by with my tools."

"No, it's fine. Just leave it all alone."

"Once a year, I don't mind. As a favor to you."

"It's not doing me a favor. I can't seem to explain that."

"If you get a guy in, he'll charge you an arm and a leg, Michèle. Think for a second."

I look at him. "Actually, if you really want to," I say, "you could clear out the gutters, too."

He peels the vegetables while I take care of the meat. It's still early, but he pours me a drink. He says, "I think you're looking well lately." I don't know how he finds that note of sincerity, how in the world he makes it sound true. He's the man who slapped me and he's the one who comes running if I'm being threatened or if I'm just feeling blue or I'm terribly tired. He's losing his hair, sure, but he's still a good catch.

"I'm not mad at you," I say. "I actually don't understand what gives me certain rights. It's reflexive, a leftover from when you and I were together. It's not conscious. Don't pay any attention."

"I didn't say a word when you went out with that violinist."

"Oh, come on. Don't play dumb. He was married with three kids, he had all the requisite qualities. But you can't say as much, right? You pick a single woman with no children, right? If I'm not mistaken."

"I didn't pick anything at all. I ran into her on your fucking elevator, if you really want to know."

"That's how you go about it? You run into girls on fucking elevators?"

"Look, I swore I would never argue with you again. I want us to remain on good terms."

"We are on good terms."

"Great. And I would like it to stay that way after this evening is over. I would like us to be on even better terms after this evening."

"You mean sort of like brother and sister? Is that what you have in mind? That we wind up being the best friends in the world?"

"Well, more or less. Something powerful, in any case."

I sort of nod. "And you thought that by having an affair with this girl, you were working in that direction? You thought you were doing the right thing?"

"I didn't think anything, Michèle. Quit it."

"You pick nothing, you think nothing. Isn't life beautiful?"

He clenches his teeth and goes back to his contentious peeling of a Roseval potato. I inwardly salute his efforts at self-control, praying he won't bite his tongue.

My mother arrives on the arm of a man my age whom I immediately identify as this wonderful Ralf person she has told me about. "She talks to me about you so often," he says. I manage a smile. My mother is wearing a short black leather skirt. She has so much makeup on that I shiver for a second as she passes the pressure cooker, afraid the steam will melt it and make it drip all over my bouillon. I'm being mean. She's not wearing any more makeup than usual. I tell her to sit down with her friend while Richard and I get things squared away in the kitchen.

"Promise you'll kill me," I say, while she strides exuberantly toward the fireplace, hips swinging—well, as much as she can swing them. Ralf toddles along behind.

She hasn't always behaved like this. She got off on this tangent gradually, as we lived through that horrible life after my father committed a massacre in a kiddie beach club while the parents were out surfing. She finally figured out that she had no other means of survival because she was not made for work. And this is what's left at seventy-five, the caricature of an aging seductress. That's all that's left. A hag. I'm exaggerating. "Kill me at the very first sign," I say.

Josie can still get through the front door but she has to turn slightly sideways and I do get the feeling she's holding her breath. The baby is a beautiful purple thing. Cold air rushes inside with them. It's snowing above fifteen hundred feet, and all that cold air is barreling down toward the plains. In a few moments, they have pink cheeks, and the collection of wine bottles is growing. We open the champagne Ralf brought and, one by one, everyone asks me who is that individual and I answer I don't know and I don't want to know.

I will never allow my mother to marry this asshole, or any other.

I hope this isn't showing in my face, or not too much. I hope I can smile at him rather than frown when our eyes meet, because I don't want to ruin the evening for so little, the dinner party I usually throw a few weeks before Christmas so I can bring together my family and a few close friends. I was married to Richard for twenty years and we always did this, at least once a year, and usually everything goes wonderfully well, except for a few inevitable clashes that can be managed or even choked off with a little goodwill and effort.

A few glasses start going around, some beer. Anna and Robert bring wine. The coat racks are overflowing. The fire is crackling. Robert tries to meet my eyes but I avoid it. Then Patrick arrives. He's alone, his wife couldn't make it. "Nothing too serious?" I ask as I hand him a drink. I make the introductions. I tell them all how we met, when he was after a prowler, just a little while ago. My mother feels it's important to have good neighbors.

Vincent is deep in conversation with his father and I wouldn't swear they're not talking about me, saying bad things, each revealing the bone he has to pick. They're so different, except for the temperamental side they often reserve for me. I think Vincent is now as strong as his father and that's a fairly upsetting feeling for me, to think that I gave birth to a child now able to punish his father. Their jaw session takes place near the fire, so I see the reflection of the flames dancing on their faces.

Sitting in the middle of the couch, Josie nurses, which for the moment distracts Robert.

Finally, Hélène Zacharian rings the doorbell and Richard springs into action, like a roebuck. All present and accounted for. And those who were getting impatient, who lifted the top off the pot for the umpteenth time to see what smelled so good, now turn their imploring gaze upon me. And all I can look at is Hélène, who has just arrived. Superb. The funny thing is, it's like Richard is embarrassed about there being so many beautiful things lumped together in one person. Anna and I exchange a glance. I know she's thinking the same thing I am, that the competition is stiff and unfair for women our age, that at times we might as well be dead.

We sit down to dinner and Patrick sits next to me, saying I was very nice to invite him and he feels honored to be sharing a meal with such a great group of people. It feels a little ceremonious, a little pompous, but I accept his thanks without hesitation because, as he says this, he puts his hand on my arm and keeps it there—which no one in the room has missed.

Robert, seated on the other side of the table, almost facing me, decides to close his eyes. And because I have no intention of provoking him, I stand up to serve, push my chair back. But my cheeks are red with the heat. Vincent gets up and walks around with the baby—whom they call Édouard-baby for some stupid reason—because Édouard-baby has started wailing in his bamboo-rayon fiber, washable diapers.

Anna has started serving on the other side while my mother claps her hands to quiet everyone down so she can talk about how good it is to be all together with family and friends and blah blah blah. Her speech is always the same until she turns to welcome the new arrivals, in this case Ralf, Patrick, and Hélène—Josie, who according to some obscure strategy Vincent had wound up insisting on including at the last minute as his new girlfriend, had already been taken care of last winter. This always takes a few minutes, these little set pieces hosted by the old bag, which gives us time to serve. Perfect. Then she turns to Ralf and, although I'm not really watching her, something gets my attention, something shiny, and she takes this opportunity to announce her engagement to Ralf here.

I burst out laughing. "Oh, sorry," I say. "Excuse me, but how do you manage to be so ludicrous?"

Her face wrinkles up but she makes no answer. Richard quickly raises a glass to everyone present around the table and, second after second, the silence I created gets wiped away, each one in turn finding some remark to defuse the tension created by mother and me. Conversations pick up, and my mother finally sits back down when Ralf signals her to with a tug on her arm, and I sit back down at my place next to Patrick, who asks me where something or other is located.

"Sorry, Patrick. Excuse me? Where what is located?"

"Your butcher."

I smile at him, more or less, but behind that mask I'm wondering. I'm not sure I really want to. Or if I *still* really want to. One should always be wary of a man who chose to make his career in a bank, I think, as I stare at the glass of wine he poured me.

We're still knee to knee at the end of the meal, but I don't intend to linger at the table. I'm neither for nor against. I'd like to be able to put him on hold. I'd like him not to hurry. He asked me what I wanted and I told him I didn't know and that this was not the place to have that kind of conversation. "And I hate whispering in a crowd," I added, asking him to put another log on the fire.

Outside, it's snow weather, just a hint of mist glistening in the crisp night air. Some of us are still at the table. I meet eyes with my mother twice, but once would have been quite enough. I know she's furious at me. I know she knows that I'm furious at her.

Anna made a fabulous pie and Josie a not-so-fabulous pie. Much more not than fabulous. Much more filling. I think she just doubled the amount of butter and flour. It's easy to see that Vincent isn't happy, but Josie is glowing, totally proud of her masterpiece, which has purplish patches.

I go over to say a few nice things to Robert before his very frustration makes him a real problem.

"Everything is fine, Robert. But I mean, I don't have to give you lessons in feminine cycles, do I? I can't right now, what can I tell you? Don't you have another girlfriend?"

"Then just explain one thing. What's all that crap with the other guy about? What kind of idiotic flirting was that?"

He's speaking in a low voice, but it sounds like yelling to me.

"Are you about to make a scene in my home, Robert? Tell me. Am I to expect that kind of thing from you?"

I put a plate in his hands and serve him a little of each pie, then wink at him and move my lips a tiny bit in an invisible kiss. Josie looks at us, then says that she used a Whole Foods Market recipe and that by the way they have an excellent panettone on sale right now. She once again sits down to nurse Édouard-baby. "Theoretically, there are no blueberries," she points out, "Just the chocolate. But I just love blueberries and chestnut cream, too." Her breasts are about the size of volleyballs. I'd be curious to know what that imbecile Vincent does with them.

Hélène comes over to compliment me on the meal and to say she sincerely hopes we can become friends. Richard keeps his distance, grinning as if he had to urinate. I actually don't dislike her, again, but this can't lead to anything, it can only lead to nothing, any way you slice it. What's he hoping for? What demented contraption, what sterile association won't a man embark upon?

"Your girlfriend is so charming," I say when he comes over.

"Oh, great. You know, it was delicious. You should come over sometime."

"Yeah, of course. But let's give it time, let's not force things."

"Listen, Richard," she says, "let us handle it. To begin with, I'll call Michèle. Right, Michèle? I'll call you and we'll go have lunch just the two of us. To begin with."

"Well, that," I say, "would be just fine with me. If we keep on like this, Hélène, we're going to get along very well."

"Fantastic," he says.

I'm stricken, but I don't show it. I can just see myself ringing their doorbell with a bouquet of flowers and a box of Ladurée macaroons. Can you really endure such a thing without losing a big part of your self-esteem?

An arm slips around my waist. It's that of my dear Anna, who has developed a very keen sense of observation and who knows what to do, depending on if I bite my lip a little or frown or knit an eyebrow or lose some color. She comes over at just the right time with her gin and tonic, which I needed very badly.

Lots of projects have fallen through these last few years. The money is hard to come by and the industry is in crisis, which is something Richard can understand. "But aren't we also paying," he says as he looks at Anna and me—and at that very moment I notice he's had a lot to drink—"for your lack of imagination, for your refusal to look ahead and your incommensurate love for all things American?"

We're used to getting severely criticized every time we refuse a screenplay, even some wildly obscene insults once in a while, and we know how to handle these situations.

We duck and dodge. My mother looks a little tipsy, too. Her cheeks are the color of ripe apricots. "Richard," she says, "you're always moaning and groaning! For heaven's sake!"

"Those are moans of agony, Irène."

She grabs his arm, and that's the right thing to do. Someone has opened a box of chocolate and it's getting passed around. When Hélène sits down, she crosses her legs and that, in itself, is a small celebration. "Don't be so negative," she says to Richard. "It's so annoying, you know?"

"I'm not negative, Hélène, I'm realistic. Taking one step off the crosswalk has become impossible."

Anna leans over and whispers in my ear, asking how exactly Richard's screenplay stepped off the crosswalk while Richard goes on with his summation, playing the apostle of difference, originality, singularity, of which he himself is a good example. "You know," I reply, "Richard is first and foremost a theorist."

Right now it's snowing without snowing. There are a few flakes spinning around, hanging in midair. Ralf is on the phone. Josie puts her equipment away. Robert stares sadly in the distance. Vincent and Patrick are seated in armchairs. I go by them on my way to the kitchen and so I hear Vincent say, "We are the people, so we're used to getting fucked."

Shorter days, lower temperatures. Winter often and for some people sets off a rise in general testiness and incredulous rage, especially, I've heard, those who draw a salary from a fast-food restaurant. I plug in the kettle. Every time I'm about to feel sorry for him, I think again of what life dealt me at his age and I stop. My mother and I weren't treated like lepers, we were treated like *dirty* lepers. Adults cursed us, children pulled our hair, bawling parents threw things at us, whatever they had handy, like the man in the butcher shop who had paid for his steak and threw it in my face.

"What are you thinking about?" my mother wants to know. I turn around.

"Oh, nothing special," I say.

She doesn't move. Head down, she nods a little, almost alarmingly. Then she looks up.

"Do you have any idea how brutal you were when you addressed me before?"

"Yes, of course. But that's nothing, you know? You ain't seen nothing yet." She giggles in bitter resignation, collapses onto a chair, and holds her head in her hands.

"He's been in prison for thirty years! What would he care?"

"I'm the one who cares. I have no father, so how could I have a stepfather?"

"I'm going to spend my whole life shaking in my boots? Is that what you have in store for me? That I just shake until the end, winding up in a public nursing home? With all those poor people and foreigners?"

"What?"

"All right. Oh, for God's sake, relax. I take back what I said."

The kettle whistles. "When Ralf is no longer around, when that whole thing blows up in your face, as expected, I your daughter will still be here. I'm a better insurance policy than he is, Mom. Objectively speaking."

I can feel a ray of hope glowing at the bottom of her heart. When she holds out her empty glass I warn her against certain excesses, but she tells me to go to hell. I fill the glass and turn to go. She wears me out. And I can hear her collapsing behind me, I can hear the sound of a chair thrown over and crashing to the ground.

So here we are on the way to the hospital. She passed out. I'm scared out of my mind. I've become her little girl again, but her face also really frightens me. Ashen, almost bluish. Patrick drives very quickly and he knows the quickest route. I'm not even sure she's breathing. I hold her hand and tears run silently down my cheeks and there's nothing I can do to stop them. Only my lips tremble a little. "Don't do this to me," I rail while we speed along, horn blaring, running a few lights, getting cursed by guys who are sleeping near the canal, in tents, in this cold. A biting, raw wind is blowing and when I pull her close to get her out of the car that icy breeze hits her in the face and she stiffens against me in a spasm and, holding on to me and twisting her face, says in my ear, "Go see him, Michèle." Those words terrify me — it's all I can do to keep from dropping her. "Go see your father," she begs me.

"What, Mom?" I say in a groan. The wind is howling around us when a fat nurse comes running, followed by Patrick and an orderly equipped with a long golden ponytail wagging and wiggling in the wind. "Mom's in a coma." That's all the news I have. I wait. We wait. Patrick has made up his mind to keep me company. I speak to Richard and to Vincent, allowing them to talk to the others and take over for the rest of the evening. I don't feel very well. Something inside me is coming apart. A terrifying shadow is hanging in the air. Patrick puts an arm around my shoulders, which is the best thing to do under the circumstances. I never thought my mother could be gone because that eventuality is unbearable, and I'm suddenly thrust into an abyss and I don't have the strength. In the past, we often worked out of a tight spot or just muddled through, by the simple fact of being together, and there's nothing to indicate that things are going to get any easier from now on. I look at Patrick. No investment banker is going to argue with me about this.

It's just about daybreak when a doctor comes along, suggesting that I go home because that's the best thing I can do. She's being watched, I'll get a call if there's any change. Instead of asking him questions, requesting information, I concentrate on controlling my breathing. Patrick holds me up. I had finally more or less calmed down during the night, but the very sight of a doctor, of a man in a medical smock, once again throws me for a loop, submerges me in the present moment. I am unable to have a normal conversation with the doctor on duty. My body no longer functions normally. He advises me to take a sleeping pill and to go to bed, assuring me that Irène's condition is stable, that he'll call me this evening. I nod. I hunch over. Patrick is there. "At least go home and take a shower, change your clothes," he advises me, putting his hands on my shoulders. I have been lying on a hard bench for hours, never closing my eyes, not knowing if she was going to live or die. Sitting up sometimes, curled up with my knees to my forehead, in any case, my arms crossed, busy trying not to shake like some poor fallen leaf. It was the darkest night of my life—well, a tie with the night my father went toe to toe with the police before they arrested him and spirited him away, out of reach of the mobs. I look at Patrick without seeing him. I put up no further resistance as he leads me to the exit. It's like drifting down a river of warm water. I don't even feel the cold outside when we cross the parking lot, gleaming with frozen sleet.

He turns on the heat, flashes me a compassionate smile as he turns onto the practically empty avenue in the wee hours.

At a red light, he touches my knee. He tries to reassure me. "Nothing is lost," he says, trying to lift my spirits as we cross the Bois de Boulogne, flooded with a bright white mist. I don't say anything.

I'm aware that he immediately volunteered to take us to the hospital, that he spent the whole night by my side, that he's been perfect—attentive, thoughtful—that only a few days before I'd found him attractive, that I rather desired him, of course I have all these things in mind. But am I still at an age to try to explain, do I still want to *force myself* to do anything at all?

When we get home, Richard is still there—which quickly answers the rather mundane question I'd been asking myself since we left the hospital, to wit, how do I explain to Patrick that I'm not going to be able to take our relationship any farther for the moment and that I'm sorry I let him believe that I would sleep with him the first chance we got.

Richard sits up on an elbow and gives me a questioning look. He knows. Richard is the only person who does know—well, Vincent sort of vaguely knows—just how much the idea of losing Irène leaves me in disarray, just how disarmed I am and certain I'll be crushed by the first obstacle thrown in my way. Irène sometimes stayed up all night and watched over me, back then, when there was danger out there, when some mother crazy with grief or something else might seek justice by taking it out on us. How would things happen now? Now that she's no longer here to watch over me?

He gets up and holds me tight. I don't object. Of all the men I've known, he's probably the best, yes, but is that enough? Is that admirable? Can't one dream of something better?

I collapse into a chair. The two men look at one another. I discover I'm not dead by how quickly I discern the rivalry immediately established between them—and of which I am the actual object. There is some—slight, halting—comfort in that. "Oh, I'm sorry," I say with a sigh. "I don't even know if you've been introduced."

They say they have been. With that, Richard thanks Patrick for being so much help to me and tells him he can go home now and not to worry. I look away. I don't want to be dragged into their little game. I'm so weary. Richard pulls me closer to his shoulder. "Oh, thank you so, so much," I say a beat too late, while he's already turning to go. "Thank you so much. I'll call you, I'll let you know what happens."

He gives me a sad, relatively touching little wave as he walks out the door into the icy air, which growls in the chimney.

"Bit of a leech, isn't he?"

"I wouldn't have invited him if I thought so. Think for a second."

"Hang on, you're serious? Are you putting me on right now?"

I laugh out loud. "My God, you're making a scene, Richard! A scene! This is the end of the world. Did you get hit in the head or something? Have you lost your mind?"

We haven't been very kind to Patrick, which is why I'm being so testy. "Look," I say, "let's not go any farther down this road. I've got other things to worry about, okay? I didn't sneak off in order to *flirt* with him all night, in case you're asking. And by the way, why on earth would you have a right to know anything? In your capacity as what? I must be dreaming."

"All right, don't start."

"Don't tell me what to do, Richard. We separated so we could live in peace with one another. I don't ask you what you do with your receptionist who's barely out of high school. So follow my lead."

Outside, the mist is lifting and the sky is clearing up. Daylight slips between the tree trunks and the almost bare branches. I breathe. As if daytime were a haven, as if I had been granted a reprieve until evening.

I run a bath. After Richard leaves, after making sure a thousand times that everything was all right from here to the doorstep, I turned on the washing machine for a third complete cycle, including soak, on the hottest setting, so that my sheets would be rid of their filth once and for all. Then I go upstairs. Marty follows me. I have locked the door behind us.

He takes up a position in the sink and waits for me to run a trickle of cool water. He's thirsty. Because he's now the only one who hasn't abandoned me in one way or another—now that Irène got into the act—I hurry up and serve him so he'll show me a little love or whatever. While he drinks and purrs—a delicate endeavor that only an old cat can master—I call Anna and apologize for not answering her messages the night before. "Poor darling," she says. "Is everything all right?"

"I don't know. I'm going to take a bath and then I'll see. I'm tired. I think it's a concussion, I don't really know."

"But are you okay? You want me to come over?"

I say I'm going to rest, that I'll stop by to see her this evening, after the hospital. That she can take me out for a drink. Even as we speak, I slip into my bath. It would be best if I could forget what Irène told me to do, not to even think about it for a second ever again, but I'm not there yet.

"I can't get over her telling you that," says Anna. "I think that's really terrible."

"And right after that, she's gone. Anna, that could be her last breath, you know? Can you imagine?"

"What are you going to do?"

"What do you mean, do? Huh. Nothing, I guess. No, there's nothing I can do. Let him rot away in prison."

She feels I'm right, that there's nothing binding about unwritten last wishes, poorly heard whispers, badly translated moans, and indistinct groans, which can't quite be made out, hardly audible and moribund ravings. She's sorry to be so blunt, not the product of the most rudimentary common sense, she's quick to add. One must grant the last wish of the dying, *to a certain degree*, she points out. Otherwise you may as well be in a cult, you may as well be that kind of crazy person. "You know I love your mother," she says, "but not this. It's over the line. Forget about it."

At the moment I'm going to bed, there's a knock on the door. It's Patrick. He's stopping by to see if everything's all right. He's off to work and wants to know if he can bring me anything when he gets back. I don't want anything, but I say thank you. He looks at once jolly and sad, seems to be waiting for something. I clutch my bathrobe to my throat while a flock of black birds silently crosses the sky behind him. "Well, Patrick," I say, "I was about to lie down, actually. I want to get my strength back a little before I go back to the hospital."

He smiles. For an instant, I wonder if he's going to jump me. Then I'm horrified when I realize that I put my short blue print robe on instead of the other blue print one, the long one, and I'm wearing nothing but panties underneath. I'm so exhausted that I went to the door dressed like that! It's too late to do anything about it, I can only make it worse by acting like some embarrassed virgin or God knows what. I tug at my belt. If I had been worried he wasn't attracted to me, this would have reassured me.

He coughs a little. "Don't hesitate to call if there's anything at all I can do," he says, putting his hand in his coat pocket to get his phone out, so we can exchange numbers he explains, and for a second I think he's going about it in a fairly strange way.

"Did you just take my picture?" I ask. "Is that what you just did, Patrick?"

He frowns, blushes. "Oh, of course not, Michèle. Of course not."

"I think you did, Patrick. Is that for Facebook or just for yourself?"

He denies it, shakes his head back and forth, and finally, as I am about to shut the door in his face in bitter disappointment, he taps "Photos" to show me the most recent shots and I recognize that it's not me, or rather it's me but I'm not half naked on my doorstep. I'm curled up on the bench in the hospital, surprised at the first glimmers of dawn coming in to bathe me in a pale communion light.

Once my surprise has passed, I can't help laughing and making a remark about how stupid I look when I'm asleep.

"You certainly do not, you're very beautiful," he tells me.

It's really very cold, dressed as I am. Every inch of flesh has bristled, every last pubic hair standing on end. I'm still buzzing from the incredibly touching tone of voice he used to make that declaration. I'm speechless.

I want to thank him for the smooth pleasure he gave me, but I don't because I don't want to encourage any more advances. "We'll talk about all this another time, Patrick. I'm freezing to death." He smiles, gives me a little wave. I close the door. I throw the bolt.

Through the peephole, I watch him go back to his car. And all of a sudden I realize that when you weigh the pros and cons of beginning a relationship, you're taking one step into old age—even two steps.

I wake up in midafternoon. I go see her—I can make out only what's visible through the masks, the tubes, and the wires—but there's nothing to see. She isn't moving an eyelash. I hold her hand for a moment, but I don't feel her presence. To put it another way, I can't feel her here. We didn't get along very well any longer. Our relationship took a turn for the worse after Richard and I separated because I had ruled out the idea of her moving into the house with me, a situation she had ardently hoped for, in order to lean on me as abundantly as I had been able to lean on her during those dark years. But though I could go a month or more without seeing her, I knew she was there. Now I don't know exactly where she is.

That fear of being unmasked, that we might be recognized and forced to face all those deaths, all that injustice, all that insanity. Thirty years later that fear is still just as tenacious, just as penetrating. Irène wound up thinking that time had carried us beyond the danger, but she could never convince me of that. Like a grown child who continues to suck her thumb, I kept the habit of being more or less on the lookout—more *less* than *more*, I guess, since I did manage to get raped like anyone else.

When I met Richard, I was on the verge of going insane. Not a week went by when we weren't assaulted in one manner or another—shoved, shaken, slapped, humiliated. I spent hours crying in my room. I even had to leave college, where I was assaulted, bullied, harassed even more than outside. Of course, they all had a brother or a sister who was taken by my father's murderous spree, or one of their loved ones had perished or been devastated. I lived in perpetual anguish and I cursed him every day, every second of every day for pulling us along with him in his downfall.

Some people let it go at conking me over the head with a book as they passed by.

I would have killed him myself if I could have. He had always been cold and distant with me, I wouldn't have missed him much. Irène jumped out of her skin when I said this sort of thing and she even punished me for it once in a while. Those words were blasphemy for her and, being as it took her a while to lose faith, there was plenty of it left at the beginning, enough to show me the lines I absolutely must not cross.

I was not allowed to want my father to die, and even less allowed to say I was ready to take care of that by my own hand. That was the devil expressing himself through me, and it earned me a shower of slaps, which I nimbly protected against by folding my arms in front of my face and remaining somewhat stoical. I couldn't understand why she went on defending him when we were enduring sheer torture because of him. I had a boyfriend and I was in love with him, the first boy I had ever really slept with, the first who meant something to me. I was sixteen and he spit in my face. That was one of the only things that ever really hurt me in life. Not only did he humiliate me in front of everyone else, he killed me socially. What pity could I have felt back then for the man who caused all the pain inflicted on my mother and me?

I wouldn't meet Richard for another six long years. Enough time to grow calloused and enough for Irène to realize that too much religion, too much moralizing had us headed straight for disaster, and that she was rather an attractive woman, if only she would make an effort, work on her appearance. She did so, with great enthusiasm, and had a few considerable successes, though unfortunately none of them lasted. Six years of chaos, wandering lost, running scared, and thinking hard. The only memory I have of that period is of a long eclipse, a world without light where I thought we would remain forever. Then one day a man is standing there, picks up the steak someone threw at my face, and sticks it right on the kisser of the guy who'd thrown it, even trying to shove it down his throat, and that man was Richard, and three months later he married me.

My father was in prison and he was going to stay there. It took me a while before I realized that this was a good thing. I had time to lead an entire life, completely new, fully renovated, while he rotted away in his cell. I'm only becoming aware of this now, but it's not enough for me to shed a tear.

I let go of Irène's hand, which sent me no signal and which my hand did not warm. Her heart is beating, though. I also remember that we were a tough team during those years, and I don't want to lose her. I knew what she was doing. I knew where the money was coming from, though she wouldn't talk about it and made up some idiotic story or another, which I accepted in the end, because it was easier.

The days are short, I leave before evening. I'm overcome by a strange sense of solitude. I stop by her apartment on the way, thinking of something else.

I open the door, and there's Ralf standing there. And so that problem comes up right away.

I meet Anna and we discuss the idea of throwing a party

for the twenty-fifth anniversary of AV Productions, the downside of which is that it would be expensive and would net us no immediate benefit. But not having one could be seen as an admission of financial strain or a sign of rebellious or crabby personalities, and none of that is good.

I've always really admired Anna's total commitment to the company we founded—in that maternity ward where the walls trembled from my screaming—sixty percent for her and forty for me. She's the executive president. She's the one who works late, evenings, Saturdays, and sometimes even Sundays. Only takes short vacations. Talks to the bankers. I've always admired her for that.

I advise her to throw the party. Just because she deserves it, because she should be proud of herself. The number of production companies that have closed down in the last few years is staggering, but AV Productions is still here.

"You never know," she says, "the wind might turn. It could turn just like that, in one day."

Anna had another miscarriage in 2001, in late August, and though her schedule couldn't explain everything, most everyone agreed that it played a big role. In fact, Robert felt that she had sacrificed their child to her goddamn production company, as he called it then and has kept calling it ever since. *Your goddamn production company. You want to talk about your goddamn production company? Don't talk to me about your goddamn production company, okay? Still at that goddamn company, huh?* Not only is it distance that saves their marriage—the distance they maintain between one another, Robert always on the road, at the wheel of his oversize Mercedes, hardly ever at home more than two weeks in a row—but also and especially Anna's complete lack of interest in anything that isn't AV Productions. She has men at her feet but it doesn't interest her, sex doesn't interest her. Not that she'll turn it down when the moment is right, when she's got nothing better to do and Robert is coming out of the shower and he's well scrubbed. But expending precious energy just to wind up in a bed under some sweaty, hairy, out-of-breath man would be asking too much of her. That's just the way she is, and she's no more interested in women. We tried it out once, during a vacation at the seaside, but we couldn't manage to stay focused and serious long enough.

It's past one in the morning when we leave her office, and the cold night once again hits me while we're striding across the parking lot. I stop. I think I'm going to cry, but I don't. I bite my lip. Anna holds me in her arms. Losing her without losing her is even harder than really losing her. Anna understands that very well. It's like I've stopped breathing. "Yeah, of course," she says, running her hand over my back.

I wind up at her place. In the fridge, we find salmon roe and blinis and it feels good to eat a little. The glass of white wine feels good, too. We speak loudly. We have another glass, we laugh.

Robert appears in the doorway, in Armani boxers, face all wrinkled with sleep, shoulders slumped.

He sighs. "Girls, what the hell are you doing? You know what time it is? You decided to go wild? Wow!"

We wait for him to turn and go back to his bedroom before we react. "I don't know what it is with him lately," she says. "He's just so unpleasant all the time." I shrug. It's high time I ended that stupid affair. Sometimes I wonder if it's not his very stupidity that attracted me. I know it isn't going to be easy, but I'm ready and I promise myself, this very evening, in a burst of new energy and a crushing need to be honest with Anna, considering that my mother's life is hanging by a thread, et cetera, that at the very first opportunity I will twist the knife in the wound by telling Robert that I've decided to discontinue our romantic interludes.

The opportunity presents itself right away. When I open my eyes in the morning, the curtains are still drawn but there is daylight. I am not at home. And that's not Marty crawling between the warm sheets and padding all over me. It's Robert's brazen hand moving up between my legs like he owns them.

I jump aside, clutching the sheet. "What the hell are you doing?" I cry out.

"What? What do you think I'm doing?"

"Where is Anna?"

"It's fine, she's gone."

He's naked. I'm wearing underwear, nervous, on edge.

"What is it?" he asks. "What's the matter?"

"We've never done this here, Robert. This is her home."

"It's also *my* home."

"Yeah, whatever. Look, I can't do this anymore. This is getting ridiculous. We have to stop. You know, Robert, I can feel things. I never spoke to you about it—of course, when did we ever talk about anything? But I have kind of a gift and I just know we have to stop doing this. I think we would grow from it."

"You think we would grow from it?"

"I'm not blaming you. You were a great partner and we'll still be friends. But it was getting to be too much to bear, wasn't it? You know very well, you can't say you don't."

"It was too much for you? It wasn't for me, not at all."

I have had time to jump into my skirt. I snap the curtains back.

"Your breasts have gotten bigger," he says.

"No, I don't think so. Not that I'm aware of."

"No question about it."

I slip my sweater on. I look around for my shoes.

"All right," he says with a sigh, "tell me the desire is gone and that'll be the end of it."

"It's not as simple as that, Robert. But all right, I'm telling you, my desire for this situation, for these lies, is gone."

"You're not answering the question I'm asking."

"Sorry. I no longer want to have sexual relations with you. Was that the question?"

"This is terribly sudden, Michèle. Give me a little time to get used to the idea."

"No, no way. That's not going to happen."

I put on my shoes, button my coat, grab my bag.

"It's like smoking, Robert. If you don't quit all at once, you'll never get anywhere. We're old friends. It'll be fine."

I give him a friendly wave on my way out. I tie a scarf over my head, turn up the collar of my coat, and rush through the bright, icy air of midmorning toward a quiet bar where Anna and I sometimes meet. The bathrooms are perfect—low light, Brian Eno music, perfume (Petite Chérie or Sous le Figuier or something), potted plants, self-cleaning toilet seats, variable-speed water nozzles replacing the toilet paper, a blast of warm air if you want it. Whatever, I needed to fix my appearance, brush my hair. It was a close call, though. I don't know how, by some miracle, I managed to pull it off. I really thought I might have to give in to him one last time, under the circumstances and considering our history, but fortunately the worst can sometimes be avoided. As men approach fifty, they get slower, grow stingingly hesitant, uncertain, even come completely unraveled. I take a careful look at my breasts in the mirror. Facing forward. Profile.

I go to the office and kiss Anna, tell her she was wrong to let me sleep—and also to have left me alone with Robert, I know it's silly, but you know very well there's this slightly uptight girl inside me and even though that girl knows that nothing could ever happen, I can't help it, even after all these years, I don't want to wake up alone in my best friend's apartment with her husband sleeping in the next room. I know, but I would rather avoid it. I know, I'm an old fuddy-duddy. No, really, it really bothers me. Anyway, whatever. I slept like a rock.

She listens to me, bemused, then tells me that Édouard-baby's father is in prison somewhere in Thailand for narcotics trafficking. "Vincent is not in debt," she says. "If I understood correctly, this guy needs money for a lawyer. Vincent is sending him some."

"You mean *you're* sending him some."

"But now it's over. I've drawn the line. Josie is pushing it, isn't she? Vincent has got some knack for picking girlfriends."

She hasn't, of course, judged a single one to be worthy of him, but I admit that with Josie he has been particularly clever, particularly sensible.

From my office, I call Richard.

"Yes," he says, "I know about it, actually. This drug thing is a total farce. That guy was just in the way, that's all there is to it."

"Well, thanks again, Richard! Thanks for going to all that trouble to keep me informed."

"What? Hang on. It seems to me I don't have any obligation to report back to you on my conversations with Vincent. So just cool it, okay?"

"You're lucky I'm not standing in front of you."

"I could come over. I can be there in ten minutes."

"Christ, how can you be so vulgar? Don't you have anything more elegant to say? Considering my only crime is asking to be kept up to date on what is going on in this family. Especially where it concerns Vincent. Well, thanks for that reaction, Richard. Thanks for that reaction. But save a little of your sweetness for your new girlfriend, don't dump it all on me."

This was the general tone of our conversations a few years ago, almost every day, before we both threw in the towel. It's a bad memory. That's the period when our first illusions got dashed, our first sour fruits tasted, our first renouncements declared. We were barely forty.

I hang up. I've learned to cut it short—nothing is worse than a conversation allowed to degenerate, getting nastier and nastier, and from which there is nothing to be gained. It's better to leave a clean, fresh wound. I'll call back later when the tension has come down. We'll cover the same ground with cooler heads.

I have a right to act like this with him. I have even more of a right now that there's this girl between us and she is breaking all the rules we set for one another to live in harmony following our separation, this Hélène. It's like he's throwing her right in my face.

I don't know anyone who likes to get hung up on. I let an hour go by, ignoring his messages, getting my notes together, making a few work calls, then I call him back. "Richard, I don't want to argue with you. Let's have this conversation again, starting off on the right foot. Please. Let's do it for Vincent. Let's try not to think about ourselves, all right?"

He answers with an eloquent silence.

"What are you doing?" I ask him.

"Who, me? Oh, nothing. You mean right this second? Nothing special."

"So I'm not disturbing you?"

"Not at all. I'm taking a bath. What's going on with Irène? I went by to see her. She scared the shit out of me, you know?"

"Sure. No, there's no news. She's old, after all. She's old *inside*. She's used up her energy. But it's frightening to see her like that, you're right. Those were your flowers. I figured as much. I changed the water in the vase."

"And are you all right?"

"Yes and no. I don't know how to express what I'm feeling, I'm still in shock, I'm taking Ativan. I'm sorry for hanging up before. You won't believe me, but I'm shaking like I'm freezing cold."

"Don't apologize. I know what you're going through."

"I know you know, Richard. And it's comforting to me that someone knows. It makes me feel not quite so alone. In any case, I'm glad you know about this thing with Vincent. At least that's a load off my mind and I can sleep well at night, knowing that you have an eye on this situation, just as much as I would have, if not better."

"What if we just decide he's old enough to work it out on his own? Anna made a mistake giving him that money."

"Excuse me, Richard. How can you say Vincent is old enough to work it out on his own? Are you joking? Has he proved anything at all? I don't know, has he crossed any deserts or sailed any oceans or scaled any mountains before he wound up in Josie's arms? So why on earth should we recognize qualities in him that he has never, as far as I know, exhibited? Just because he's our son? And so that would make him smarter than other people?"

"Well, yes. Why not?"

I don't forget that he thinks he writes the best screenplays in the world—his work for TV, he says, isn't worth speaking of. I've often seen him brooding at his desk after getting a refusal or finding the object of his dreams returned by regular mail, and I never made out even a hint of self-doubt. And more than anything I loved that strength he embodies, that self-assurance he exudes, while all I wanted was to crawl under a rock, curl up in total darkness, and not even dare to mention my name ever again.

"What would you say," I reply, "about a mother who just watches her son barreling over the edge without lifting a finger? Just to see if he's a big boy who could work it out on his own."

Silence is all the answer I get. But I can hear his breathing, and the water flapping in his tub. Outside the weather is fine but the wind is blowing pretty hard, roaring against the windowpanes and the trees getting twisted every which way.

"Don't take everything I say so hard," I tell him with a sigh. "I know you think what you're doing is for the best. But you don't know him that well. Well, I mean, you do know him well, but you assume he's strong, you ignore his weaknesses and you send him off to slaughter."

"To slaughter? Your choice of words, Christ!"

"Your son is slinging french fries at a Mickey D's, Richard. Maybe it's time you opened your eyes."

"Selling french fries at the age of twenty-four never killed anybody."

"But it appears that now he has a wife and a child to look after. Do you see the difference that makes, or don't you? Look. Bringing up a child means going all the way, you don't just stop in midstream. And I know you're going to tell me that at his age it's not leaving him high and dry, that it's time for him to strike out on his own, but just consider for one second the possibility that he has walked into a trap. Try to picture that. You wouldn't help him? He won't listen to me anymore. But you, can't you explain to him that she is *not* his wife and that her child is *not* his child? Can't you get him to listen to reason?"

"Look, I think he's old enough to see to his own business. That's what I think."

"No, hang on. What are you saying to me, Richard? I don't follow you."

"You understand me very well."

"Am I to understand that you're not going to do anything? That you're just going to stand there watching? What is wrong with you? Have you gone crazy, too? Are you doing this on purpose?"

This time he's the one who hangs up. But because I anticipated his reaction, I don't feel a thing. It's not as stinging, no, not quite an exclamation point.

I look outside, the trees on the avenue, the black monolithic Areva Tower, the wind over the rooftops, the tiny passersby all bundled up, leaning over, the race of clouds across the sky. It's only a few days before Christmas. The hardest part is holding still and watching the disaster happen. Knowing but doing nothing. We will live to regret it, that much is obvious.

I grab a few screenplays and go to visit my mother. In the lobby, I buy some magazines and two mixed salads. On my way up in the elevator, I realize that my mother can no longer read or eat—or speak, or walk, or bat her eyelashes (which she used to do so well). I hide a twitch of sadness with my hand.

You never know, so I read to her for a while. The Old World continues to decline, offering its soul up to evil bankers. I admit I'm a little afraid that she'll suddenly wake up and be all over me about whether or not I've honored my so-called moral obligations regarding her dear husband.

Did she honor hers by living life hell-bent for leather, violating every moral code she could? What atrocious maneuver did she not try to get me to go see my father? What contemptible low blow did she not use to bend me to her will? This severe concussion thing stands out only for its disgusting perfidy and its lack of concern for others.

It's midafternoon but it's starting to get dark. An airplane crosses the sky, leaving its trail of white in a gentle curve toward the setting sun, veiled in milky orange, its back end breaking up, little by little, then disappearing entirely in the blue. "You can't stay mad at me," I say. "You know it, you can't pretend you didn't know." The salad is awful, full of much-too-salty black olives. Somebody came in today and fixed her hair and I feel guilty.

I can't stare at her for too long. Otherwise I start crying. But provided I only glance at her, never looking too long at her face (the skin of which looks like cardboard), provided I only glimpse her briefly, never lingering, then I can stand the act of sitting by my comatose mother, holding her cold hand, waiting for who knows what while gazing out the window. Late in the afternoon, they start hanging colored balls and tinsel in the hallway. "There is no way I'm going, Mom. I don't know if you can hear me, but there is absolutely no way I'm going. He's nothing to me now. I'm ashamed of the part of me that is linked to him, don't make me repeat it over and over again, five hundred times. I didn't blame you for visiting him all those times, I let you do it. I respected your point of view, now you respect mine. Don't force me to do something I find unbearable. You're his wife, I'm his daughter. We don't have the same take on things. You were with him by choice. Not that I blame you, you couldn't have guessed. But not me. His blood runs in my veins. You understand what the problem is? I'm not sure you do. I don't think you ever really put yourself in my shoes. The very fact that you demand such a thing of me proves that you have never put yourself in my shoes *at all*."

I stop talking when a male nurse comes in to see if everything's all right.

Ralf gets there when I'm on my way out. He takes the opportunity to speak to me once again about his staying in Irène's apartment. "Just don't burn the place down, that's all I ask," I tell him. "Apart from that, we'll just wait and see."

Ralf is a mystery. What exactly is he after? Unless he's got a thing for old ladies, I don't see what he expects from this affair with my mother. I don't get the feeling that Irène is an uncommon sexual partner—though I can't deny she has considerable experience. Richard advises me not to worry about it. "You're right," I say. "I really shouldn't. So, fine, we don't invite him over." It's better that way. I don't even speak of Hélène's presence at this family dinner, but I certainly have a thought or two. I let Richard do what he feels he has to. He has a soul, a conscience. He's free to choose, so let him choose. We have a drink at a sunny but miraculously sheltered café with the snow that fell overnight shimmering in crystals on the sidewalks. It's not very cold. "But we could invite Patrick and his wife," I say. "What do you think? A little new blood. They're nice."

"He's not *nice*. He works for a bank."

"Yes, I know. Well, let's say I'm using my joker. Let's try to make it as cheery as possible. Please. Let's think about something new."

He takes my hands and rubs them with his, but he knows that I will never forgive him for having slapped me, and that these little acts of tenderness—stroking my back, holding me to his shoulder, massaging my ankles, and so on—are now performed with a sigh. Not so long ago, he said to me, "Three years, Michèle. Almost three years, over a thousand days. Can't we—"

I interrupted, "Certainly not, Richard. You're dreaming. Not everything can be absolved, unfortunately. Even if I wanted to, I couldn't. No one can do anything about it, Richard. We just have to accept that."

I absolutely abhor this display of sentimentalism that comes over both of us, here and there, at the evocation of a memory or upon having a drink, making us, stupidly, almost maudlin. Stupidly, because completely without hope of improvement. No hope for individual redemption, no chance to remove the stain. In that sense he's like my father, that inclination to be condemned, their irreparable acts banishing them, precluding forever the possibility of reprieve.

But he's been feeling much better lately, much more accepting of the fact that he is responsible for our permanent breakup because he raised his hand to me, then let it fall hard against my cheek. He's much more accepting of the fact that since he's met Hélène he's lost me forever. I really think he's not going to die of sorrow, that this girl's effect on him is akin to a powerful antidepressant.

I take my hands back, the sun is still shining. His whining isn't quite so heart-wrenching since he's been sleeping with her. He seems slightly fresher, in better shape, you can tell by the way he's smiling at me now—I had forgotten that he could smile like that—by the patience he is showing. It's really depressing. This girl comes along and she gets only the good stuff. I order vodka. I smoke a cigarette.

Richard makes some food suggestions, I nod, hardly listening. I haven't had much appetite since Irène has been in the hospital. I've even been a little nauseous. I hope I'm not pregnant. Only kidding. I mean, how could I be? Besides getting raped, my sex life has been dry as a desert for a while, which it hasn't been for him, that much is obvious.

Mom dies during midnight mass. We have left the table, opened the presents, started drinking Bollinger already and we don't regret it at all. It's an amiable family moment. Outside, despite the neighborhood being covered in snow, the weather is practically warm and some of us step out for a smoke. I thought there might be a little tension between Anna and Josie, but Anna quickly had a few drinks and was soon in high spirits—so much so that she actually went over and caressed Édouard-baby's cheek while he slept in his mother's arms. The sky is clear and full of stars. Rébecca, Patrick's wife, is a short redhead with chiseled features—she pronounces the stars gorgeous. He then informs us that she was baptized only a few months ago, at her express request, following a mystical experience she had while visiting the Beauvais Cathedral, and that she would very much like to watch a few minutes of the midnight mass if this didn't bother anyone. "No, go right ahead. Just turn the sound down," I say. At that very moment my phone vibrates in my pocket.

At first, I can hear nothing. Distant crackling. I get up and walk over to the front door, asking the person to repeat what they said, it's a weak signal. I walk outside. I say, "Yes? Hello?" and that's when they tell me she's dead. I don't know what to say. I go, "Oh?" and I hang up right away, set my phone not to take any more calls. I shiver.

For a second, I think about calling the hospital back to make sure I heard right. I sit down in a wicker armchair she gave us when Richard and I moved into this house and it makes the horrible groaning noise I want to make, but I remain silent. For a second, I clutch the armrests and wait for the earthquake to be over. When it's over, I'm clammy, my temples are moist. The moon shines splendid over the woods, Paris shimmering in the distance. A hedgehog crosses the garden in front of me. I can hear the hum of conversations. I turn around and see Anna and Vincent having a smoke on one side, and Patrick on the other with Robert, who has found someone to whom he can explain the perfect science of the cigar.

Everything is where it should be, all peace and quiet. No one has noticed a thing. I force myself to slow my breathing, to contain my heartbeat.

I stand up. I smile with no trouble. I ask them if they want anything, then go inside laughing at a remark Robert made and of which I did not understand a single word, but I act like everything is perfectly normal. They don't notice a thing. I go inside. Rébecca is sitting on the couch with her legs crossed, staring wide-eyed at the silent images of midnight mass. The three others are standing around the fireplace with drinks. I sit down next to Rébecca.

"I just found out that my mother is dead," I say, now also staring at the live feed from Notre-Dame Cathedral.

She looks at me and merely nods. I don't know where she is exactly, but she's not here, not sitting next to me. I smile at her. By confiding this awful news to her, I have loosened its grip. And at the same time, I have maintained control of it. I don't have to share it with the others and Rébecca sure isn't going to give me away. I ask her if she wants some herb tea or a slice of ice cream cake. She's thrilled about both. I take her order. I had remembered her as sort of strange and diaphanous, but nothing like this. I go into the kitchen for the herb tea. As I go by, Richard gives me a little friendly wink, and if he can't tell, if nothing seems out of the ordinary to him, then the camouflage is excellent.

When I come back with a tray for Rébecca, the others come inside, bringing an odor of frozen earth with them. The conversations start up again, eyes meet, and very soon I am gently floating among them, my terrible secret clutched to my breast like a warm talisman.

At dawn, I close my door on the heels of Robert and Anna, last to leave, and I feel like I have won Irène—and myself—a few hours' reprieve, that we had enjoyed them, spending a last few moments together, on the sidelines, the two of us, alone like we used to be, with no one else to count on, and I am extremely glad. It calms my nerves. I remain on the doorstep a few seconds, waiting for them to leave, waiting for Robert to find the keys to his car. A blackbird lands a few feet away from me and from the way he cocks his head and eyes me, all full of bluster, you would think he and I were old friends, that we both knew very well what it was all about. Before I go up to bed, I cut him a few slices of apple and serve them to him in a small plate.

I wake up in midafternoon and start to spread the grievous news, getting my share of embarrassed silences and wishes of courage to get through this ordeal, offers of help of every kind, but I don't want to see anyone and I manage to get rid of all these would-be generous souls.

Except for Patrick. His visit has nothing to do with Irène's death—which he doesn't know about yet. He's here on a search-and-retrieve mission, the object of which is a certain chain bracelet that has no particular value but that Rébecca brought back from a pilgrimage to Lourdes. "I'm sorry, but she's absolutely freaked she might have lost it," he says, trying to squeeze his hand between the seat back and the cushion of the sofa where his young wife lounged all evening. "Thank you so much once again for a wonderful Christmas Eve," he adds, even as he continues fiercely searching, knees bent, brow knitted, one arm into my cushions up to his biceps. I wave off his thanks, even as I observe the man kneeling at my feet. When I opened the door he was standing there with the mist floating all around, and I could hear barking far off, as if he had crossed through cotton.

It's only four but there is little light left. How many times have I done it right there on that couch, with Richard, or with Robert, or with that violinist or whoever else, over all those years?

"And bang, there you go!" he says, brandishing the bracelet and smiling from ear to ear.

My crotch is approximately at the level of his nose, about

three feet away. Naturally, I'm not wearing the wrong bathrobe this time. I have the long one on, but I let it cautiously loosen in front. I wait. He keeps smiling and doesn't move. I look up and admire the snowcapped firewood in the blue light of evening, then I figure time is up and I turn around to head for the door. "Irène left us this morning," I blurt. "Sorry I can't invite you to stay for something, Patrick, but I need to be alone. Give Rébecca my love, would you?"

He rises, seemingly tripping over several sudden emotions, but Irène's death seems to win the day and he backs off. He mutters some feeble apologies and kisses my hands, but it's too late if he's thinking sex now, things I was thinking less than a minute ago and that now have unfortunately vanished in my mind—there's no controlling these things.

Our offices are closed between Christmas and New Year's, so I use those few days to see to terrible matters—funeral arrangements and sorting through her things.

Losing your mother over the holidays is particularly hard because the funeral parlors are on a skeleton crew and a varnished unreality of suspended time and numbness is added to the pain, making the passing of the person who carried you in her womb all the more stressful and incomprehensible.

Ralf promises he will move out before the end of January. That's a long way off, but I let it go. I can easily understand that he can't just find another place to live in two seconds, so I accept it. We work out a few times during the week when, disturbing him as little as possible, I can come over and start going through Irène's things, putting them in boxes.

I dart a quick look around the apartment, just to get an idea, I tell him, of how big a move I'm in for. I make him aware of the funeral arrangements I've made as well, in case he decides to attend.

I've hurt his feelings. The idea that I could think for one second that he might not come to Irène's funeral has wounded him deeply.

"I only meant that you have no formal obligation, Ralf, but you are welcome, you know that."

I discover the quick temper I hadn't seen in him before. Richard says it doesn't surprise him, that he had a feeling the second he laid eyes on him. "That slightly forced smile of his, you could just tell. A real pain in the ass."

"Yes, you're right. But he was sleeping with her only a little while ago. That counts for something. He's not some distant cousin. He held her in his arms, he kissed her, rubbed himself against her. It's sort of horrifying."

"What's horrifying?"

"What's horrifying? Well, I mean this relationship they had, how he knew her, their age difference, their intimacy. It's awful, you know? There were two things she wanted. She wanted to get married again and I was opposed to it. Totally. That's the first thing. The other was about my father. She wanted me to go see him at least once before it was too late and he completely lost his head. Which I refused to do. What do you think? All in all, it's not a pretty picture, right? I figure Ralf might be the last person who gave her pleasure—it certainly wasn't me, anyway, and I'm awfully ashamed, horribly sad about that."

We're strolling through the tombstones on display,

browsing the coffins. On the other side of the street there's an RV dealer with weathered pennants flapping against a gray sky. Richard gives me his arm. I hope Hélène will wind up seeing that things between him and me aren't that clear and she'll finally explode. And just watch, everybody will be looking at me, criticizing *my* attitude. As if I forced him to do anything whatsoever, as if I forced him to keep me company. I think he knows what he's doing. And if he doesn't know, then I'm very sorry.

Be that as it may, I'm glad I have him here because my head is spinning and it turns out I am incapable of making *choices*, of *deciding* on one model or another, on which lining, and I beg Richard to do it for me, whatever he feels is best, while I step out for some air and even smoke a cigarette.

The burial is Thursday. The sky is white, a few snowflakes swirling in the slightest breeze, sticking to the polished sheen of the coffin. I am flanked by Richard and Vincent. I can feel them ready to launch into action should I give out in the least. I don't worry about whether there's a nearby chair in case I start to go wobbly—I'm in good hands.

I can't make it all the way through, I don't have the courage. I don't want to watch the coffin get lowered, but I don't want to interrupt the ceremony. I motion that all is well and that I don't need any assistance, and I walk toward the exit. I take a few steps, then I faint.

When I come to, I'm a little down the lane, on a bench that has been cleared especially for me. I am not surprised. It is a terrible shock. The groundskeeper, who has seen it all, advises me to eat a lump of sugar. I'm his third fainting this week. I sit up. I reassure the people leaning over me.

I'm as white as a sheet of paper, I'm told. Probably, but I'm fine now. It was a fairly difficult moment. You always think you're stronger than you are, and this is what happens, or so I tell them. Reality sets you straight.

Patrick is the one who takes me home. I've been declared unfit to drive and it's either get tied to the backseat of a car or give up the idea of getting behind the wheel, after the demonstration of self-control I just gave them, crumbling amid the tombstones like a frail wisp of nothing.

I'm in a fairly dark mood. I would so much rather go home alone and not say another word until dawn of the next day, but they practically carry me to his car, sitting me down inside, fastening my seat belt, leaning into the window to tell me to be still until further notice. I avoid Robert's ardent glare, which has become a worrisome nuisance.

"Don't make conversation," I tell Patrick as soon as he pulls away. "Thank you."

We drive along the river, cross over it, then through the wood, and I never so much as glance at him or speak a word. He doesn't make a sound, drives nice and easy, through a dusting of snow that is starting to darken the sky. "We got lucky," I say.

"They say there's one hell of a wind coming tonight. Better close your shutters."

I nod. His company is not unpleasant, but speaking is really painful. And the truth is, I find him exasperating. That constant lag, the missed beat between us.

When we pull up, I don't wait. I get out. He still hasn't driven off when I get to my door. Now that I have a better idea of what his wife, Rébecca, looks like, I'm more forgiving of him. Speculating on prices for vital resources, drilling down to the level of new financial systems probably doesn't require exceptional humanity or uncommon sensitivity, but is a life with someone like Rébecca something one can truly wish on anyone?

I shrug and I go inside. I turn off the alarm. I look outside but I can't see him anymore because it's suddenly snowing very hard. I put the heat up before I went out this morning, so the house is comfortable. It feels bigger now that I live alone, but it was perfect when Richard and Vincent lived here, and even better in the beginning when Irène was staying with us. I had fixed up a room under the attic, a place for me to work, with a desk and a few cushions and a big-screen TV. Irène had part of the ground floor and it was a little cramped in the end and she finally drove us so crazy that we decided to pay the rent on a place *somewhere else* before there was any bloodshed.

I bought the house about twenty years ago, after the unexpected success of one of our first projects, and I keep it in good shape so there's at least one good solid thing in this family, so it will remain standing, so that not everything will have been in vain. It's been termite-proofed. A few tiles flew off the roof in the storm of '99 and we decided it was a good time to renovate the roofing. Richard never liked it much because he couldn't stand the idea that he owed these walls and this roof to my talents only.

I never managed to chase those considerations from his mind. I finally gave up. In the end, I forgot that everything unresolved pops up again sooner or later, even sharper than before, and that hurt festered between us to the last.

I go up to the attic to see how much space I have for Irène's things and I use the opportunity to spy on my neighbors across the way. The snow is silently cascading. A few strings of Christmas lights are gleaming in the downstairs windows. Smoke rises from the chimney. Pale clouds darken the sky.

I'm not very hungry but I decide to go downstairs and eat in order to get my strength back. I put some earbuds on and I listen to Nils Frahm's album *Felt* while I break some eggs over a frying pan, a cigarette stuck in the corner of my mouth. Mom is definitely dead this time, no doubt about it, yet Nils Frahm does finally, completely win me over.

There's a real storm blowing now and it's hard to know if it's the weather or the time of day that's darkening the sky. I can hear the wind howling right through the earbuds.

I put on pajamas. I remove my makeup.

Night has fallen when he comes over to say that he doesn't feel right seeing all my shutters open in this weather. "I didn't want to disturb you, but I thought this is so silly. Half her windows are going to get blown out unless we do something." I hesitate a moment, then I let him in. We have trouble getting the door closed. He looks me up and down. This guy has a knack for bursting in on me when I'm dressed in odd ways. "You should've seen it in '99," I say. "It was the end of the world."

But I have hardly finished my sentence and he's already at the first window, throwing it open, grabbing the shutter against the wall outside. He must now wage a merciless battle against the elements. He bends over, hair standing on end. He grunts. I think about leaping into the raging swirl that has already caused a little stirring around in the living room, but thank God he manages to get the shutter closed and all is quiet once again. "Patrick, I have never counted, but I think there are about twenty windows in this house."

"The wind is from the west. Let's take care of this side first."

He is brimming with the authority he often lacks in other circumstances. I obey him, following him to the next window. He puts his hand on the handle. I give him a signal. The icy wind whips inside. While Patrick handles the window, I lean outside to grab the shutter and pull it back toward me with all my might. It slams. "Perfect," judges my charitable neighbor who has quickly closed the window behind me. I stand there stock-still a moment, stunned by the whole operation. He reaches out, rubs my arms through the soft and delicate fabric of my pajamas. The length of his arms—a couple of feet—is all the distance between us.

"Let's go check upstairs," he suggests, as I gather my wits and wipe the tears the wind brought from my eyes.

My bedroom is on the west side. He stops outside the door. Gives me a questioning look. I lower my head and nod. We go inside. My bed is a mess, my underwear is tossed on an armchair. I wasn't expecting anyone.

"I wasn't expecting anyone," I say, following his eyes. He makes believe that he's discovering the window, which is moaning and crackling in the wind blowing the snow toward the city. By this point, he has covered part of the ground toward me. At this point, he can win the day if he wants to.

He seems to think it's better to first take care of the window and we pull our moves again. This time all that air in my lungs leaves me a little groggy. I sit down on the bed for a second to catch my breath. He sits down, too. He puts his hand on my knee, caresses it through the soft and delicate fabric of my pajamas.

"Let's go check the next floor up," he says to me. "We've almost got it done. You hear that? Seriously, can you hear that wind? This is your bedroom? I like it. Did you do the decorating?"

He rises. We go up to the next floor. My office. I don't turn the lights on. There are the gigantic cushions. The western window has swollen from the humidity so it takes the two of us to turn the handle that opens it in the center. When it finally comes open, we both go flying onto the floor and he winds up on top of me, lying right smack on top of me, and I can feel an electric current in the time before he leaps to his feet to close that damn shutter and that damn window through which that damn wind is blowing.

Only the attic left to go. I don't mind. There's an unusual atmosphere up there, full of things we haven't touched since they've been here and that represent all that remains of what we were before, of what concerned my mother and me. Trunks, boxes, papers, photographs, never unpacked, never opened, never looked at. We climb up the little staircase. Up there, the wind is roaring like an airplane engine, the roof beams squeaking for all they're worth. It's fabulous. I turn on the light. The lightbulb blows. "Oh, shit." We go in anyway.

Now I am on the lookout for the least little sign, but he

goes straight for the window and starts shaking the catch like crazy. When it opens, I'm in position and I lean outside to get the shutter. Then I let out a desperate yell, shaking my butt in my flannelette pajamas. "I can't, Patrick! Help me!"

I think it's a little much to rely on me to make the first moves and I promise myself I will bring it up to him later. I find it a bit humiliating. Do I need to tease him to show him the way? Do I have to take his hand and put it between my legs? Whatever. I manage to close the shutter and Patrick suddenly comes up from behind and rubs himself against my back while he sticks his hand down my pants, held up by a mere elastic band, and straight down to my privates.

I was beginning to think we would never get there. I sigh with satisfaction, I spread my legs and twist my neck around for a kiss, but he leaps backward, lets out a sort of whine, and scampers off into the dark toward the stairway, hurries downstairs. It takes my breath away.

I have a very bad night. In the morning, I find flowers outside. I put them directly into the garbage.

At about ten, he rings the bell. I cut his explanations short by telling him that I'm not interested, and I close the door. I watch him through the peephole. He has walked away about ten feet, hanging his head, looking glum. He plops down on the porch glider, the cushions of which I had removed, and rests his forehead on both hands.

At noon, he's still sitting there in the same position. The sky is clear, the wind has died down but it's still regular, and it's bitter cold. Would I be at all responsible if he snaps right there outside my house and I didn't lift a finger to help? I go on with my day, going upstairs and down, and from time to time I double back to make sure he hasn't gone, and that imbecile is still at his post.

Anna calls me and I bring her up to speed. She advises me to send Patrick home as quickly as I can, so he won't catch cold or make a scene. "How on earth do you get into these situations, anyway?" she asks me. "I can't get over it. You want me to come over?"

"No," I say after glancing outside at Patrick, "that won't be necessary."

I watch a movie with Leonardo DiCaprio and when I look up it's evening and he's still there. I pace around impatiently awhile longer, then I finally get dressed and go outside.

I stand there in front of him, fists on hips. "What are you doing, genius? Are you going to stay in the glider all night long? Tell me." There's maybe a spark that flashes in his eyes, but that's all. He's gripping the collar of his camel hair to his neck, his hand seemingly soldered to the lapel of that overcoat, now glazed in white by the cold. I can sort of tell he's making a pitiful attempt at a smile, but the muscles of his face are apparently stuck.

I slip one arm under his elbow and force him to stand up. He isn't very willing, trembling to the bone, completely hunched over and distraught. I sit him down on a stool—with no intention of keeping him long—in front of the fireplace and make him a hot toddy which, as soon as he recovers the use of his fingers, he will be able to consume. For the moment, he can only shiver.

"What exactly is your problem, anyway?" I ask, "What's wrong with you?"

I don't expect him to answer. I smoke a cigarette. He shakes his head. I can tell he's trying to form words, but nothing is coming out of his mouth. I offer him a throat lozenge with a mild painkiller.

"Drink your hot toddy and go on home, Patrick. Let's leave it at that, all right?"

His teeth chatter a little more, then he says he only wants to apologize, tell me how disgusted he is with himself for laying his hand on me.

I look him over for a moment, quaking in front of the hearth.

"All right, it's okay. Don't make a big deal out of it."

I light another cigarette and slip it between his lips. "Tell me the truth, Patrick. You're not attracted to me?" He is so indignant he practically retches. He stammers. Night has fallen.

I watch him. I don't say anything. I think I've lost patience. I'm tired. I wait for him to get a little color back, until he's finished drinking his toddy, then I see him outside, pointing him toward his car, parked out front. He turns back to me twice, pounding his chest, and I give him the slightest of nods. It's a full moon. I watch him pull around on the black ice and up in his driveway across the street. I have met some weird guys in my time, but Patrick takes the cake. Still, in spite of it all, I like him. Part of me wants to give up on the whole thing, right away, completely and immediately cut it off, because getting involved with such a complicated and unpredictable man can only mean trouble. But I guess I'm not very old yet because I feel I still have a few unusual adventures left in me, I still have the capacity and the propensity. I imagine this game can't be over so soon.

I sit by the fire awhile, my mind wandering, then I go upstairs to my office to wrap some presents. I'm late — Mom's death has wreaked havoc on my plans. I write a few cards, slip them inside, then I yawn. I still have my hand over my mouth when someone comes up from behind and hurls me down onto the floor, which is carpeted. In our fall, I grab the wire from my lamp and the room is suddenly dark. I scream. I get hit hard in the jaw. My attacker is wearing a ski mask. I'm a little stunned but I muster all my strength and scream even louder. This time, either he went about it the wrong way or I'm just completely off the charts, but he can't quite hold me still. I have no fear, my fury is a black hole, I don't even know if he's armed or not, that's how blinded I am by anger.

He does, however, fall on me with all his weight and gets hold of me around the neck. Screaming "Help! Someone help me!" has earned me a good, hard blow right in the face but my rage is too great for fainting. While he tries to get his pants down, I latch on to the base of a bookshelf stacked with books and I manage to squirm out of his hold, turning, kicking from my back and hammering at his skull with my heels.

But he regains the advantage and I'm forced to retreat, expecting him to rush me again. I'm sitting on the floor, back to the wall when, by chance, my fingers close on the scissors I had been using to wrap my presents. He lunges toward me again, his hand up to grab me, but that hand gets stopped, pierced in midair, stabbed through and through with a wild thrust of my seamstress scissors.

Now it's his turn to scream, to make his voice heard. But I already know who he is—perhaps I have always known—before I tear his ski mask off.

I leap to my feet, scissors pointed at him. "Get out of my house," I tell him. It's an order, issued in a hushed voice trembling with rage. "Out of my house! Out!" I wave the point, all red with blood, in front of his eyes. There are flames shooting from my eyes. I'm spoiling for a chance to come at him again. I will be quick as lightning. I am that furious. He can see it, and I'm glad he can see it. He grimaces, backs away in panic, holding his injured hand close. But behind that grimace, I don't know. I don't know what he is really feeling. He rushes down to the front door. "Get the hell out!" I yell, "Don't ever come near me again!"

He turns and grabs the door handle. The most troubling thing for me is taking this out on Patrick. On the Patrick I know, that is, the one who is my neighbor, who flirts with me and all that. It was obviously not that Patrick who just assaulted me—that guy in the ski mask is not him. If he didn't have that wound in his hand, my confusion would be endless. I'd be telling myself, "What on earth are you doing? That's your friend, Patrick. Don't you recognize him?"

The door opens. He's backing away. I follow him with my scissors still pointed at him, face high. The full moon is practically blinding. I blink. The two Patricks then overlap in my mind and I stop. He keeps backing up and now I can see his double perfectly, the one who raped me once and who has just tried to do it again. He slips on a patch of ice and falls to the ground. I have to stop myself from going to help him, a reflex reaction.

It occurs to me to call the police, but I don't. I'd rather take a bath. Even to myself, I don't dare say the truth.

The next day, I go get my car, which gives me a chance to visit the cemetery for the first time. There's no obligation, it could wait, but the place is relatively deserted so I can beat it out of there if I choose to.

The stone hasn't been set, but that little mound of earth is perhaps even more shocking. Someone left a few flowers, which haven't wilted yet, and this period between Christmas and New Year's is always very strange, which is proved by this uncommon silence that accompanies me, producing a feeling of unreal calm, one that suits my mood to a T. I lean over to fix something or other and I ask her to forgive me for that poor showing I made the other day at the funeral. This is a beautiful day to go visit your mother's grave. The sky is clear and white as a lily and the air is just the right amount of nippy.

I straighten up and realize there are lots of trees around, and lots of sky. "This is a good spot for you," I say. "You're in the city, but it's like being in the country. You'll have birds and bees in summer."

I put one hand on the black and ice-cold earth. Then I turn to go.

The sun is setting when I pull into the minimart for cigarettes and cat food.

I'm glad I got through that cemetery ordeal, glad I held

up. That's one less thing on my mind. I have made an honorable showing in the face of that shock, I'm getting through it better than I expected. I know now that I'm going to be able to come back here once in a while, without histrionics. I still need her. I come out of it reassured.

I meet Patrick on my way into the store. His arms are full of groceries, but he freezes when he sees me, goes white, then suddenly starts to run—probably afraid that I'm once again armed with something or other—and as he bounds away, one of the bags gives out and its contents splatter on the ground.

I go on my way without turning around, walking toward the spirits. I'm still furious at him. I'm furious with myself as well for letting myself be fooled, for not seeing what was right there in front of me. I retain an option of bashing him to bits with a bat or whatever, just to render him harmless, to render him lifeless. That's still a possible scenario. He better not come near me.

But I still want him. It's atrocious. I would let loose a scream of anguish and despair right now if I weren't afraid I'd wind up handcuffed to a radiator by the security guards with shaved heads. I hate this horrible trick I'm playing on myself. What is wrong with me? Is it age? Perplexed, I collect some club soda, gin, olives, fat-free *fromage blanc*. For a second, I wonder if it might be better to get back together with Robert, concentrate on that relationship and ignore the rest. It would simplify things, snuffing out the embers that still glow inside him, but I can't quite persuade myself and I give up on the idea.

"I didn't send your friend an invitation," he tells me as

he welcomes me to the New Year's Eve party, hair impeccably combed, a scarf around his neck, spiteful smile, white teeth.

The first man who gave me pleasure looked like him, except I was sixteen. He was the psychologist who saw to me after my father's killing spree. He was a well-known psychologist, a scumbag.

"Robert, listen carefully. I am very happy that you didn't invite him. Very happy."

"Well, well."

"I'm telling you."

I hand him my coat. I'm not crazy about spending New Year's in his company, but I couldn't get out of it, the others are here. I'm not in any shape to spend New Year's Eve all alone.

I buried my mother only three days ago. I don't expect to be overflowing with energy, or dancing on the tables, but I feel that a little company is necessary. And maybe a drink, too. Irène loved this kind of party. She would start preparing for it a month in advance. Richard just mentioned that, and he is after all the person most affected by Irène's passing, next to me. She was not a very easy woman to love, but Richard was used to her and time wound up working in his favor. After only a few years, they had become good friends. He, himself, couldn't care less about the life of depravity she led.

She often suggested I could be more like him. When it came to respecting other people's lives. Or advocated submitting to his mediation. Or following his advice. He offers to help me sort through her things and I say yes.

"Patrick not here?" he asks.

"No, I don't know. Why do you ask me that?"

"Why?"

"He's married. He has a wife. Why do you ask *me* where he is?"

"Oh. Well, I'm sorry. I just thought…"

I shrug and walk away from him. There are a few writers at this party, a few filmmakers who have done clips for us. There is so much ego in this place that if ever there was a blackout they would all just start to glow. They all seem well, they have billions of projects but they're mostly here to relax and enjoy the party, to forget about the business for at least a few hours out of the year, and all you have to do is stick out your hand and a glass of champagne miraculously appears.

"Oh, Vincent, my darling, thank you. How are you? Josie isn't here yet?"

His face scrunches up. He pours himself a glass of champagne. "She isn't coming. She won't set foot at Anna's."

"Really? How did that happen?"

"It just did."

"Wow, everything's so complicated. Anyway. So are you happy with that flat-screen?"

"Yes. I mean, yes and no. It's on all day long. I wonder if she ever takes a leak."

"She'll ruin her eyesight, that's for sure."

Anna motions me over, tells me that it's better this way, for Josie and for her, and that she's counting on my support with Vincent. "You know, the girl is a real menace and that imbecile just can't see through her."

"I warned him like a hundred times," I say. "A hundred times I cautioned him. A hundred."

"She wants to get the father of her child out of jail. That's all she cares about. She'd go to any lengths. And if Vincent can't find the money, I don't think she'll be in love with him much longer. You know, I think we should be thinking about the issue of custody, avoid any nasty surprises."

"Yes, but not tonight," I answer with a smile. I turn toward the party.

I'm not a man, but looking at Hélène I can almost imagine what they feel in the presence of such a well-turned-out young woman. "I'm thinking the same thing you are," says Anna, a hand on my shoulder.

I light a cigarette. They have pushed the furniture back and set up a big buffet table. I mingle left and right, avoiding Robert.

But later, at about three in the morning when everyone is fairly exhausted, he manages to corner me near the bay window where I stopped to gaze out at the falling snow, silly me.

"I'm going to make an announcement," he whispers in my ear. "It's time to stop lying." I immediately grab him by his lapel. I know he isn't bluffing. I know that look in his eye. "Fine," I say through clenched teeth. "Fine. You're pathetic, Robert."

"No. Wait, take back that 'You're pathetic.' Take it back right now or I'm going to."

"I take back the 'You're pathetic.'"

"I just want to remind you that fucking me was not always the chore you make it out to be lately."

"Talking about the past won't help. Don't ask me to explain what's inexplicable."

"Don't talk to me like that. I'm not a moron."

We set aside a late afternoon in the coming week. The snow has almost stopped, the lights are glistening.

"Aren't you disgusted with yourself?" I ask him. "Having it end like this?"

"I would've been happy if we kept it right where it was. Never changing a thing. With you still the same person."

"And so blackmail is all you could figure out? Fucking asshole."

"Take that back."

"I take back 'fucking asshole.' But this is beneath you, Robert, you can't change that. So I'm sorry if my heart isn't in it the next time we meet. Don't be mad at me, respect is something you can't control."

Be that as it may, I accept the drink he offers me but I refuse to drink it with him. "Fucking me is one thing…" I say.

He laughs and turns around after doffing an imaginary cap to me. I'm aware that my conversation is a little ridiculous, but I'm just about seriously drunk. Great. That's exactly what I wanted. Exactly what I needed.

At about four in the morning, I disappear without a word. The streets are deserted. I stay off the main thoroughfares and after a while I'm out of town. I get to within a few miles of my house, into a patch of fog that's starting to play tricks on me. I have to brake a little sharply, twice, because I can't see a blessed thing. I'm supposed to have fog lights, but when I turn them on the results are less than conclusive. What inevitably had to happen then happens: I miss a curve and wind up in a ditch.

The impact is fairly hard, enough to deploy my air bag, which nearly knocks me out. When I recover, the engine has stalled and the first thing I notice is the silence. I reach out and turn off the ignition and now I'm in total darkness.

I know where I am. I'm in the woods. I'm almost home. It's not far, but it's a narrow road where there isn't much traffic, even during a business day. Suffice it to say, the new year is starting off great. I throw my head back and stay there a moment, unmoving. Then, as I'm about to get out of the car, I let loose a scream, loud enough to shoot chills through the sleepy surroundings in the milky darkness. Excruciating pain in my left ankle. My mouth hangs open in agony, in pure astonishment.

Then I catch my breath and lean over cautiously to touch it. I can't see a thing. I'm in a panic over the idea that I'm going to discover my ankle has been mashed or my foot has been severed. But no, it's all there, and apparently there is no blood. The only thing is, I can't move.

I think it over. I turn on the hazard lights. The fog is so thick I can hardly see the hood of the car. I let loose a big sardonic laugh. I think. I'm a little dizzy. I admit I've been a bad girl. Which inspires a feeling of evil power. I call him. I ask if I'm waking him up. I explain my situation.

"I'll be there in ten minutes," he says.

I light a cigarette. Reason only very rarely wins out—and it only engenders frustration, boredom, and desperation when you give in to it, or so I tell myself.

He just threw an overcoat over his pajamas and his

hurrying practically warms my heart, but I don't show it. He leans over. I roll down the window. "Take me home. Thanks," I tell him. He nods, hands in his pockets, staring at the tips of his shoes. We stay there like that, completely still, for a full minute. Then I say, "All right, Patrick, look. I'm hurt. You have to help me to get out of this car, can't you see?"

He's lost the power of speech but not the use of his arms and I hold on to him as he lifts me out of the car and out of the ditch. This is the first time we've made physical contact since I tore his mask off and I am having a very strange, very violent reaction. He is practically carrying me. I'm relatively fascinated. By him, of course, but also by myself, with respect to this gift I have for carefully picking them.

He puts me inside next to him and suggests I put my seat belt on and not once do I manage to meet his eyes. He keeps his fingers tight to the wheel, in plain sight—and he is in profile, in the feeble light of the dash, never once turning toward me.

I say nothing. I recognize the smell in his car—church incense. I was in it once when the man who drove it was a charming neighbor and not the madman who had raped me a few days earlier, and I remember having smiled at recognizing that smell from my childhood and how soothing it seemed. It doesn't make me feel that way now. I find it ghoulish. I open my window. Icy air rushes in, but he doesn't say anything. He's concentrating on his driving. That bandage is soaked in blood—I figure his wound opened as he struggled to get me out of the car. That's probably to remind me just how brutal were the events he and

I lived through, only a little while ago. I must not make the mistake of forgetting that. Patrick is a violent man. He didn't hesitate to punch me in the face, grab me around the throat, twist my arms up behind my back hard, smother me, and I will be covered in bruises this time, too.

And strangely, I'm not afraid of him. I'm on the lookout, but I'm not afraid.

I don't know how on earth he can drive because you can't see anything at all. The mile and a half we have to cover is like an ocean of foam into which it feels to me like I would have sunk sooner or later, considering my current state.

That last glass of gin I had for the road, right before I left, that wasn't a good idea.

My ankle is swelling, I can feel it. I struggle to bend over—which is how I make the delightful discovery that my muscles ache all over. The ankle feels warm and shapeless when I touch it. He remains stuck to his steering wheel, tamped down inside himself, head between his shoulders—unless it's because of the cold air rushing into the car, but I need to breathe. I forget to tug on my dress.

Then all of a sudden we're there. I can't see the house but it's very possible and Patrick does seem sure of himself. He even gets out to make sure, then comes back nodding in the affirmative.

Once again, I have to explain that I'm not going to make it on my own, that I'm freezing in my seat, before he finally moves his butt over to pull me out of the car. I put one arm around his neck, aggravating his discomfort, which I can feel as it forms and grows in the mind of my one-night-only savior at the instant we touch. I'm glad I can provoke such a reaction in him, glad I possess that little sprinkle of power.

He carries me. I didn't ask him to, but I never let go of his neck and I expected—correctly, it turns out—that he would sweep me off the ground, through the front yard and up to the door, where I give no indication that I would like to touch either foot down anytime soon.

I rummage in the pockets of my coat for my keys. I ask if I'm too heavy, but I don't hear his answer.

I open the door, turn off the alarm, motion for him to carry me upstairs. "You know the way," I add.

I think he's in shock. I think he doesn't understand. I think in his present state he would agree to cleaning out my cellar or tidying up my attic before he leaves, all I have to do is ask.

He puts me down on my bed. Right away, paying no attention to him, I nervously take off my panty hose and toss them. By pure chance, they land at his feet. Then I pull my ankle up toward my eyes for a better look. It doesn't look great. It's already pink and swollen and shiny and it hurts like hell. I look up, grimacing, and I'm thrilled to see that the sight of my bare legs, my white thighs, my dark lace—my gymnastics have put it all out there on display, I'm not hiding anything from the eyes of this discriminating connoisseur—that this delicious display, the baring of which, as I said, provides me with a none-too-negligible inward satisfaction, leaves him petrified.

I stretch my leg out toward him, thus exposing even more of my crotch, ostensibly so he can take a look at my ankle and give me his considered opinion or God knows what. And I wait. I'm ready to blast him with incapacitant agent if I've made a mistake—my Guardian Angel is under the pillow. My leg is starting to cramp when he decides to back away, his eyes locked on the part of my anatomy he covets but which, once again, he decides to forsake. He lowers his head all at once. For a moment, I maintain that somewhat obscene position, fairly unambiguous, but it has no effect on him. He soon scrambles toward the door and scampers down the stairs.

Marty jumps up on the bed and rubs against me. I pet him.

Later I go downstairs, having wrapped my ankle in a skin-tone Ace bandage, clutching the banister, hopping step by step, and I lock the door behind him. I have no cold compresses, so I use a plastic package of frozen peas. The fog is gone, the sky is clear. I call a tow truck to get my car and I take two Alka-Seltzers. It's the first of January.

I get a phone call from the prison. My father has hanged himself overnight. I sit down, but in fact I'm not thinking anything at all, I'm hollow. Leaning over the kitchen table, forehead resting in one hand, my phone vibrates in the other. A journalist, who wants to know if I am indeed the daughter of the man who slaughtered the children at the day camp beach club in the '80s. I don't answer. I hang up.

I wanted to be a journalist when I was sixteen, the year my father splattered us with blood. I wonder what kind of journalist I would have made if I'd had a chance to pursue my studies. I stand up. I let my phone vibrate on the table.

I'm ashamed of my feeling of relief. I'm ashamed. I wish I could at least offer up a pang, some fleeting frown, some regret as compensation, but there's nothing doing. Rather, I'm worried this whole thing will crop up again — a mud rising from the depths. I wonder if that is his revenge, his punishment, if he used his last breath, his last few moments of lucid thought, to rain thunder down upon me because I never once in thirty years took the time to visit him, as he complained to Irène. Because I deprived him of the comfort my company might have provided, the support of his child.

I can hardly remember a thing. I have vague memories of photographs I've seen of him — especially those the newspapers kept printing over and over again for months, but I can't make him move in my mind, I can't hear his voice or smell him. So without those elements, the fixed images are nearly meaningless and sterile. I've forgotten him. He's an empty chair. Over the years and with no regard for the agony he caused us, Irène kept her little flame burning, as tiny as it might be, by way of several stories she told that featured him in a positive light — your father did this or your father went there — but it was a waste of time, she was wearing herself out for nothing. Your dad said this, your dad said that. I would nod, I would just move my head and never heard a word of what she told me.

I think Irène kept a whole box of photographs. They're not in the attic, I didn't want them, but I imagine she kept them, tucked away in her apartment. Photographs of him, apparently, from his childhood until prison, which Irène had managed to hide from the press, dozens and dozens of photographs of the Monster of the Aquitaine at every phase of his life. She was offered a fortune, they would have been stolen from us if she hadn't left them in a safety-deposit box, while my mother and I went homeless for months, moving from boardinghouse to hotel, on and on.

It isn't late, the sun hasn't reached its apex. The frozen peas have helped my ankle regain a nearly acceptable appearance. I tie my bandage snugly and, brandishing a cane, I take a few steps around the room for practice while I wait for my taxi. It's a fine day, the snow in the garden has bright hard crystals at the surface.

I give my mother's address. On the way, we pass the tow truck winching my car up out of the ditch.

I go inside. I walk toward the study, which Irène had converted to a walk-in closet, and I start opening a few drawers when Ralf comes up on my heels, hair all mussed, wearing only boxers and a T-shirt. He shakes his head, upset. "Oh, no, Michèle. Come on, you can't do this."

I turn around toward him. "Hi, Ralf. What's the matter? What can't I do?"

"This. Just showing up, letting yourself in without ringing the bell."

"You know I have a key, Ralf. I don't have to ring the bell. You shouldn't have bothered, I'm not staying long."

"That you're not staying long doesn't change anything, Michèle."

"Of course it does, it changes everything. Don't be unpleasant."

"No means no. Sorry."

I scratch my temple a little. "Look, Ralf, I came to pick up some important documents. I can't wait for you to buckle your suitcase, it needs to get done now. So let's not make a big deal of this, all right?"

He waves his hands and shakes his head in protest and just then an entirely naked brunette woman, about half the age of Irène, comes up behind him and juts her chin out toward me to ask who I am. I don't say anything, I ignore them.

I finally get my hands on a shoe box, full of photographs that I identify at first glance, and I close it back up right away, as if some fumes of hell might come wafting out of it. Then I jump back into the taxi, which is waiting in the icy sunlight.

The daylight has started to wane. I don't bother to take off my coat. I go straight to the garage for a shovel and walk outside behind the house. Because it hasn't been very cold for very long, the earth isn't too hard. Then I get some denatured alcohol, empty the box over the hole, soak the photographs through and through, light the fire.

I don't go as far as putting out my hands to warm them by the flames, but I can feel the heat on my face and I close my eyes for a moment and listen to the reedy hiss of the flames and I stay there long enough, I stay long enough to be certain that it's all been reduced to ashes, shivering in the cool evening. Then I fill the hole back up and tamp the earth with the shovel while a crow crosses through the sky, balefully cackling.

Irène would have had a fit. I remain outside a moment, leaning against the side of the house in the pale dusk and the odor of burnt paper. There was never a time when she stopped seeing him. She kept in touch, maintained a physical link to him, which regularly gave rise to spectacular clashes between her and me, mostly toward the beginning, but which never stopped her from making those goddamn visits. Still and all, God knows she never hid the rancor she felt toward him, considering the life he left us, one of paying bills and getting insulted, running away, etc. She kept going back to see him again and again, which made me absolutely furious at her and which she could never quite explain. She remained voluntarily muddled. She would never have forgiven me for burning those photographs. I can just hear her accusing me of killing this man a second time—which seems impossible.

I think again of her last request, that last gesture she expected of me, and that just shows how she remained attached to him despite the aimless life she led between visits, when she would generally show up with a scarf around her head and a skirt with a hemline below her knees. I'm angry at her for thinking that her stroke might melt my resistance and usher me down a road of indulgence. Is that all she thought of me?

I have a message from Robert. I call him back. "Hello, Robert? I was going to call you. About tomorrow, actually. Could we reschedule? It turns out I can't walk."

"It's no problem if you can't walk," he replies, "we're not going on a hike." His implacable logic leaves me speechless.

I'm not in a fantastic mood when I show up for our appointment. He's already in bed—it seems to me that the hair on his chest has gotten even a little whiter since our last roll in the hay, during which that detail had already struck me and completely knocked me out for an instant. "Whatever else, Robert, don't expect anything complicated out of me. As you can see and as I told you, I'm not going dancing or jumping around the room. And Anna and I have had a rough day, into the bargain. See, the holidays are over."

I put down my cane and start to take my clothes off. "I can't get over how you have gone about getting me into bed. Just don't come complaining afterward. When I've lost all but my last ounce of respect for you, don't come complaining."

I don't turn away when he tries to kiss me on the mouth, but I'm like a lifeless doll. It's already dark outside and the room is lit only by the lights of the city. I've always known I'd wind up regretting falling for him. *So here we are*, I think, *it's done*. And I think of the work I brought home from the office and how I should be taking care of it right now rather than doing anything else. It'll take me half the night as it is, if I never stop to eat.

"Relax," he says to me.

"I'm not a machine, Robert. You can't just press a button."

It's his move. After a minute, I'm beginning to wonder why I'm making this all so complicated while Robert is there with a certain level of mastery concerning my body and appears relatively sane. But I don't have the answer.

I try not to let my pleasure show because I don't know what strings it comes with. It isn't easy. I taught him everything and he was a good student. I clench my teeth so as not to bite my lip.

We have two gin and tonics sent up when we're done. I get out of bed and limp toward the bathroom. I use a chamomile body wash and I clean myself thoroughly—

having the scent of another person on me has always disturbed me.

He comes in to comb his hair. He's nude. He looks at himself in the mirror.

"You were fabulous," he says to me. At first I think he's kidding—I went completely inert while he rode me like a rodeo—but he's as serious as serious can be. "You provided some very special sensations," he goes on. "How did you hit on that idea of playing dead?"

I look at him for a moment without answering. "Anyway, whatever," I say. "You see, I'm as good as my word. You got what you wanted. Fine. Let's stay friends."

"Of course. I totally agree."

I look him over for a few more seconds and decide it would be useful to stipulate that remaining friends doesn't mean having sex.

I don't take calls with blocked caller IDs, in order to avoid journalists, penitentiary officials, and anything even remotely related to the death of my father. Regarding the funeral, I decide not to lift a finger, to play dead once again though in a different context. Even if that means picking up the tab when it's all over.

Richard supports me. There is no need to explain to him why I'm acting this way. He knows, he saw what it did to me when we first met, in what condition my father had left my mother and me by slaughtering those children. I think I might have gone insane if I hadn't met Richard, if he hadn't watched over me so carefully during the years when I first came up for air—somber, wan, and scared stiff. Watched over me while I learned to live again, made me a child so I could get my feet back on the ground, find some peace—I'm not sure, by the way, that I found any peace at all in Vincent's birth; I didn't notice it if I did.

"It's incredible that your mother died on Christmas Eve," he says, "and your father on New Year's Eve."

"Yes, I noticed that," I answer.

Sympathetic to my plight, he holds me in one arm. I break away before he sheds a tear on my neck. "We weren't supposed to live with other people," I toss out. "It ruins everything, you know?"

He looks down. Breaking his word is heartbreak for him. I'm thrilled to be his guilty conscience.

It probably has something to do with the holidays, but I see him often these days, just as I run into Hélène fairly regularly and I can just imagine what stream he's carried away on, what intoxication he just could not resist. I know what he's looking for with me. I know what excitement and what anguish wash over him lately, because I lived with him for twenty years and I can see how he behaves with her, how his eyes give him away, expressing the painful thirst he has for her. But I can't help it. I can't help this terrible, laughable absurdity that rules our lives.

Our son Vincent is a good example of where this dangerous road has led. Now he's had a fight with the manager at the McDonald's during a meeting and he's lost his job. That is going to put a serious crimp in his ability to pay rent, for which I am listed as guarantor.

It's cold and sunny, the traffic is moving, the tops of the cars capped with snow. Josie hasn't lost an ounce, she might even have gained a little. The apartment is small, with a fairly low ceiling, so she seems huge to me—two hundred pounds, Richard tells me, and he's more up on these things than I am. He's come as an observer, being that he can't weigh in on financial matters because his resources are so scant.

Josie has made scones. A dozen of them. As soon as we're seated, she takes one and swallows it in one mouthful. While Vincent is holding out Édouard-baby to us for the customary kisses and compliments, she makes another one disappear in the same manner—as if by magic.

"Some things are unacceptable," he explains. "True, I wasn't thinking about my rent. But in that case you just stand there and you let some asshole walk all over your life. Is that what you want me to do?"

"That's not what your mother's saying, Vincent," Richard chimes in.

"He knows very well that's not what I'm saying."

"You're not saying it, but that's what you're thinking. That I should have shut my mouth."

"What about your pride, darling?" asks Josie, staring dreamily at the scones. "What could you have done with your pride?"

Richard coughs into a fist, trying to create a diversion, but I pay no mind. "Josie," I say, "when one must support a wife and a child, pride becomes a luxury. I thought that when he took this job, Vincent understood that. I thought he and I had discussed it thoroughly."

"Excuse me," he says, "but you're the one who hammered this into me, don't you remember? Never let them walk all over me, always stick up for what I believe in. Did you forget? That little flame I must always keep lit?"

"I never told you not to think, Vincent. Besides, I always told you to think *beforehand*, not *afterward*."

"I can't let him call me a dirty little Jew without reacting."

"Well, for starters you're not Jewish. No one's asking you to carry the weight of the world on your shoulders. There are millions of jobless people out there. Thirty million in Europe alone. That's a lot."

"Your mother is worried about you, Vincent."

"I'm worried about myself as well," I say.

I shouldn't be afraid, but I am, because this weakness, instability, this precarious situation is suggestive—it takes me back to the dark years my mother and I went through, when we didn't know how we would make it through tomorrow, whether we would have a bed to sleep in and food to eat once my father was convicted and thrown into prison for his crimes. I don't feel I can go through another ordeal like that. I really don't want the hard times to come back.

"All right, Vincent," I say. "Fine. Do the best you can. We'll see what happens. Let's cross our fingers."

Satisfied, Richard feels obliged to massage my shoulder with a tender hand. He has been so frightfully sentimental lately. The demise of my parents has apparently rekindled his protective instincts toward me.

"Fucking trust me," says Vincent. "I won't have much trouble finding something better."

I look at him but I don't answer because I don't want to douse his enthusiasm, which I love for its purity and naïveté. I would love to find such innocence again myself, once in a while, to be certain my powers remain intact, that nothing is insurmountable, everything is possible.

There are only two scones left on the plate Josie is sliding toward us. Neither Richard nor Vincent nor I have touched them. She asks if she can kiss me. I nod, though there is a piece of pastry still stuck to her lip.

The burden of an extra rent is not good news for my finances, but I put a good face on it and I let them compliment me for my generosity, my indulgence, my kindness, and all that. I use the occasion to ask after Édouard-baby's father, the one who is in prison, using the generally euphoric mood to bring up a topic I wouldn't have known how to broach in other circumstances.

For a moment, they're thrown. Richard once again clears his throat in his fist. "How is this going to work?" I ask, keeping my tone breezy. "Seems to me, a child can't have two fathers."

Obviously, I'm not interested in the fate of the biological father, nor in the reasons that brought him to where he is today. I only want to know what they are planning to do and, just as I feared, they haven't planned anything at all.

It's better to leave. It's better to leave than to have a falling-out with them, better than saying things you'll regret later but will remain etched in stone. Anna isn't surprised. She came to the same conclusion before Josie decided she would never set foot in her house again. And although Josie never convinced Vincent to follow her example, she did manage to reduce their time together and Anna can't forgive that extremely grave low blow.

The snow that fell this morning has stuck and the

temperature has dropped. There is an icy wind blowing. I came home early because of the traffic hazard warning—heavy precipitation is forecast for tonight. There is whitish smoke curling from his chimney. Over a cup of piping-hot tea, I watch him go back and forth carrying logs. He's lucky, I think, his secret is well guarded. I haven't turned him in. I could send him to prison or to a loony bin, but I'm not going to. He's lucky he's dealing with me. He should come over here and kiss my feet.

The woods nearby are white. I look up at the sky. Shimmering brown clouds break up and scatter as the wind picks up. Evening comes. I call him to close my shutters. After a few moments of silence, I ask, "Have you gone deaf?"

I have to force myself to see his *other*, the one hiding within, the one behind. It's so much effort it's nearly impossible. I'm practically wondering if it was a dream.

"How about that ankle?" he asks, already rushing to the nearest window, just like the last time—though for the moment the wind isn't nearly as strong.

"My ankle is fine," I reply. "Thank you. How's your hand?"

He shrugs and smiles, resigned. "Nothing too horrible," he assures me, rotating it side to side on its axis, like a puppet.

I follow him in his duties, going from window to window throughout the house and at no point does he make a move to even come near me, at no point does that jovial expression leave his face, at no point can I make out his *other*, not even a trace, not even a fleeting glimmer, and I haven't taken my eyes off Patrick, not for one second.

Does a demon dwell within a body twenty-four seven, or does he only drop in for a moment? It's a question I've asked myself about my father. Sometimes I lean one way, sometimes the other, always convinced I have just now found the correct answer.

He hurries home—he's alone, with Rébecca on her way to Compostelle—to get some eggplant caviar he bought in the Marais, which I'm supposed to flip over. I watch him run outside and meet the rising storm. It isn't snowing yet but the sky keeps getting heavier. A pearly halo comes off the moon. Meanwhile, I mix a couple of Black Russians. Then he comes racing back down, swept along like a wisp of straw in the gusts of wind, zigzagging this way and that, but ever making his way toward my door, which I open, letting him in. He's out of breath.

I am astounded by my behavior. Patrick himself doesn't seem able to figure out what's going on. He stands there in the foyer, struck dumb and smiling, an almost painful smile that seems to ask what's wrong. He waits for me to tell him what comes next. I'm astounded. Now it's my turn—apparently there is another Michèle.

"Let's see about this eggplant caviar," I say, turning around.

There is no way it's dinner, an invitation to sit at the same table like we were old friends, to *share* a meal, to act as if nothing has happened, but there's no denying I called him. I'm the one who asked him to come over. And honestly, I can hardly believe it. I want to pinch myself.

I hand him his drink. He hands me my piece of toast. "Delicious," I say. The wind starts to roar in the chimney. I still have a few memories of a time when the use of amphet-amines was widespread at exam time or under pressure, and I literally have that same sensation at that precise moment—an electric current shot through me from head to toe, my face stuck in spider silk, my palms getting clammy, my mouth drying up, my thoughts coming fast and furious.

"Well," I ask, "how was it?"

I don't recognize my own voice. He's kneeling near the coffee table, seeing to the toast, then stops in midspread and looks up at me. He looks back down and shakes his head, like he just heard a good joke.

When he's all done squirming and manages to look back at me, the *other* appears to me for a second, frowning and terrifying, and I'm about to grab the poker to keep him at bay. But he disappears and it's Patrick again, touched, sitting on his heels and looking at his drink, which he picks up and finishes in a few quick sips.

"Was it good? How was it?" I insist, with a smile so forced it looks like I just tasted something sour. "Answer me."

If he could lower his head any more, I'm fairly sure he would.

"Well? Did you like it?" he forces me to repeat in a low voice.

He looks up at me again. There is that touch of madness, sure, but he's still attractive and, when he feels like it, his eyes are pure poison.

Now the wind is howling, ample and deep, and you can feel the pressure on the walls. "It was necessary," he finally affirms.

I don't react. Those words get etched inside my head.

I light a cigarette. I am entirely thrown by his answer. And furious as well. My eyes dart around the room with every issue battened down and I give myself quite an earful for being feckless, arrogant, stupid. But I'm not afraid of him. I turn my back on him to adjust a log, I'm not afraid. When I'm finished, I ask him to leave my home.

"Right now," I add. And when he stays there, dumb-struck and smiling—apparently he's the dumbstruck-and-smiling type—I point my Guardian Angel at him and I warn him, I won't say it again.

He understands. I probably used just the right tone of voice, probably had just the right expression of resolve on my face, practically foaming at the mouth. I see him to the exit, pointing my spray can at his eyes the whole time. I am so tense that I am practically trembling and I can see that he's worried about my nervousness, fearing some uncontrolled or rash act. I'm experienced with this kind of equipment, although I did once inadvertently trip the spray mechanism and one joker almost lost an eye.

When he opens the door, we remain there stock-still in the whistling, howling dark of the garden. With a frown, he seeks my forgiveness. God only knows how long you can stay standing in that storm.

"Get out!" I say through clenched teeth.

I am very upset about the way I've reacted to this whole thing, about the confusion it's caused in me, seemingly more unimaginable and obscure with each passing day. I hate having to struggle against myself, to wonder who I am. Not having access to what is buried, buried so deep inside me that only the tiniest, vaguest murmur can be heard far away, like some forgotten, heart-wrenching, and totally incomprehensible song—that doesn't help matters.

A few days later, Anna suggests we hire Vincent and of course that would also be a way of solving the problem of his income, but I'm not sure about it at all. I did have the idea, but I gave up on it because, first of all, I'm not at all sure Vincent would be able to handle a desk job of any kind, but also because he told me to mind my own business and hung up on me. Things are a little better between us now that his father is living with another woman, but I'm not certain that's enough.

Anna brushes my reticence aside.

"Well, in any case," I say, "I'm not going to be the hardest one to convince."

Josie will go ballistic, that's easy. Anna answers that she would just love to see that.

As for Vincent, he maintains it's only temporary and he will talk sense to Josie, make her appreciate the climate of uncertainty that reigns high and low in the Old World.

I don't know. I don't want any confrontations. I'm being cautious. I'm thrilled that things are looking up for Vincent but I'm nevertheless wary of having a professional relationship with him—an experiment that turned out to be very disappointing with his father and me, only making things worse between us.

"He won't be in your way," Anna says, trying to reassure me. "He'll be my responsibility. I'll find him a desk somewhere."

I think she really is trying to wipe Josie off the board.

I can feel that exuberant fury coursing through her, that dark desire to have someone to battle, to measure herself against—and with each passing year she only gets stonier and more pugnacious, and her spoiling for a fight just sharpens, overshadowing the rest. I observe her, intrigued. I can see how she has Vincent coming and going, her web growing around him. I can see the stage being set for the coming battle. I am very glad to stay out of it. Let them complain about my lack of enthusiasm—too bad.

The storms of these past few days have taken some trees, broken a lot of branches, and a truck full of wood stops in front of my house one early morning and, while two men unload it and stack the logs behind the house, Patrick tells me not to thank him, that we couldn't just let all that wood rot, and blah blah blah. He blinks in the clear morning air and smiles on my doorstep. He adds that it's heaven sent.

Any excuse, apparently, to keep our relationship alive after each of our despicable encounters—but sometimes, I tell myself though I don't believe it, even things that start out terribly wind up falling into place surprisingly well in the end. "I think we should have dinner," he says to me all of a sudden, staring at my doorbell.

"No," I say, "that's impossible."

He takes a moment to recover from this, then peeks at me with one eye. "I meant I'd take you out to dinner, not at my place."

"You have a sense of humor," I say, "a great sense of humor."

For three days, I don't even see him. His chimney is smoking from morning to night, there are lights on inside but I can't make out any movement. I have other things on my mind, I can't worry about Patrick's schedule, but it happens that I'm working at home—which allows Vincent's arrival at the AV Production offices to happen without my worrying about it, about finding him a spot, making the introductions, showing him how the copier works, the finer points of the coffee machine, and so on. All things that would have very quickly driven me up a wall.

In my office at home the worktable is at the window, with Patrick's house right across the way. The best view is from the attic, but this window is quite sufficient. I am here to work, not for anything else. Yet any movement—someone leaving, coming home, a car door slamming—immediately gets my attention, forces me to look up. And for the last three days there is nothing moving at all besides the evening lights getting turned on and the wisp of smoke from the chimney. It's a still and silent winter tableau, a slightly tedious one.

On the morning of the fourth day, coming home from my practically one-legged run, I take a detour past his house and catch my breath, hands on my hips, overheated and frozen stiff.

The dusting of snow from the night before has erased every track and footprint around. The weather is fine, the silence punctuated by cries of birds.

Nothing is visible inside—the curtains have been drawn. I ring the bell. I turn around to look at my own house across the road, and I blink. I ring the bell again, no answer, so I walk around back. His car is in the garage.

He is dead drunk. I find him collapsed in the living

room, unconscious, after having carefully slipped in through the kitchen door, one step at a time, calling aloud, "Hello? Hello!" while the clumps of snow from the soles of my shoes melted in shiny little puddles at precise intervals on the parquet floor.

I open the curtains. There are empty bottles strewn all around.

It's evening when he comes over and rings my bell, to apologize for that pitiful display and to thank me for dragging him into the shower and deservedly blasting him with cold water and for making a pot of strong coffee. I didn't stick around to see how he managed, but he's wearing clean clothes and he shaved and combed his hair and, were it not for that pale complexion, he could go back to his bank right now and no one would hesitate to entrust his life savings to such a nicely turned out and likable guy.

"I get the feeling you don't really get it," I say. "But that's my fault. I have only myself to blame. It isn't easy, all right? I'm going through a hard time right now, I feel a little lost. So you should take that into account. If I haven't been as clear as I should have been, I'm really very sorry, Patrick. But take that into account. You know, sometimes people would do just about anything to feel a tiny bit better."

Before I can make a move, he gets one foot inside, presses his lips to mine, and backs me up, kicking the door closed behind him, and we are sprawled on the floor in the very spot where he raped me the first time, and we are grunting and groaning and fighting like dogs in an alley.

He pulls up my skirt, rips open my panty hose, and grabs for my genitals while I hammer him with my fists and try to bite him. Then suddenly a veil is torn, the path is lit before me and I immediately stop struggling, lying there inert and consenting just as he is about to do the deed.

He is lying on top of me. He hesitates, stiffens for a second and moans, then collapses like a soufflé.

Then he leaps to his feet and races outside, not even bothering to close the door behind him. I stand up and do it for him. Marty, who once again has been watching the whole thing, stares in surprise as I go by. "It's a little complicated to explain," I tell him as he tags along behind.

During the next few days I don't think much about these events because I have lots of work and I'm out of the house very early and get home in the evening, and I have neither the strength nor the will for any adventures. I sort of glance toward his house on my way out. The shutters are closed, smoke rising from the chimney, all is quiet. I do the same thing on the way in, I see his windows lit, nighttime sparkling on the snow in his garden, but nothing more. I pull into my garage, turn off the engine, find my keys, and stop thinking about it.

In life, work is actually the simplest of things and I can get used to the fatigue that accompanies the endless meetings, endless phone calls, and endless rereads and so forth, just as long as I can come home at night, whip myself up a sandwich, hole up in my bedroom, get undressed, run myself a bath, smoke a little grass to relax, listen to music while playing with my glycerin soap. Alone with my aging cat.

Originally, Marty was supposed to be for Vincent, who for months had been begging us to get a dog. Richard wouldn't hear of it and figured a cat would do the trick, but

Vincent wouldn't even pick him up. In the end, the kitten found safety in my arms.

I'm glad I have him with me. He's not much help when I'm being assaulted, but so what? At least with him I don't feel like I live in an empty house. I talk to him. And we have no mice.

Vincent's arrival slows our work, of course, because he's often getting underfoot, looking for a pencil or a stapler or waving to us from behind the glass because he wants some question answered about the archiving assignment he's been given, just until we figure something out. I tried to argue the point—this was no time to be training some-one, we had to play catch-up on certain projects, we were behind schedule—but Anna was too much in a hurry to put her plan into action to be bothered listening to me. So my days are long and busy as it is, I have no intention of adding more stuff.

Especially since things soon get ugly with Josie demand-ing that Vincent immediately give up the position Anna found him just when he needed it most.

"So she doesn't know what a permanent position repre-sents?" I ask with feigned indignation, in order to quickly quash any suspicion that there might be, given my pathetic neutrality, some secret agreement between Josie and me. Anna smiles in the shadows while Vincent nibbles on his thumbnail. I consider bringing up what an absurd rush he had been in to throw herself at this woman's feet, despite all our warnings.

Richard has gone to flirt with Hélène for a few minutes, and when he comes back down he inquires about his son's decision. "Well, buddy, what do you say?" Frightful suspense. Then Vincent looks up to Anna and says he's staying. Anna is very happy. I recognize that look of unabashed joy that Vincent inspires in her at times, the first of which was when she carried him up to the baptismal font. I poked Richard with my elbow, pointing out the picture of pure happiness she embodied.

She suggests we all have lunch. I say we can't, we don't have the time, but it's three against one—then four, because Anna tells Richard to go get his new partner.

"Oh," I say, "is that what you call her? Are they getting married?"

She shrugs. "They're together, right?"

"Quit it, Mom," says Vincent with a sigh. "You know that very well."

I light a cigarette. When they arrive, I look elsewhere.

A few suspicions do nevertheless persist concerning Vincent's ability to stand up to Josie. Still and all, he looks determined and he's even thinking about spending the night at a hotel if he can't get her to listen to reason. I steal glances at Richard and Hélène. He and I used to be a couple. Now he and another woman are a couple. We're in the middle of the meal but I'm no longer hungry and I order a gin and tonic.

When it comes, he turns to me and gives me a look.

I pay the bill for my father's funeral. A few articles appeared, noting his death and recalling the massacre, but apart from the string of insults posted in the readers' comments nothing has gotten back to me—not a phone call, no contact of any kind, until Ralf remedies this oversight.

"Just one last maniac," he says to me, "if you don't mind me saying so."

I'm packing up Irène's clothing for the Red Cross. I pause in my duties, explain in a pleasant tone of voice that no decent man would go around insulting a dead man in front of his daughter. Then I basically ignore him, getting back to my task.

"Stop putting on airs," he says, "I could never stand that crap."

"Have you been drinking?"

"I never could tolerate a prig."

With that, he caves. December is a month when men get drunk—they kill, rape, form new couples, recognize children who aren't their own, run away, moan, die—but at least this one can still talk and in the end I learn that long ago we went to the same school and he remembers how the whole country was horror-struck by my father's deed and, even at the time, he couldn't stand me because I was so stuck-up. I can't remember a single face from those years, perhaps what he's saying is true.

"Go take a shower," I say. "You don't smell good."

He gives me the evil eye, shaking his head a little. "One less asshole in the world, anyway. And I'm glad I fucked his wife."

I don't answer. I slip on my coat and gloves. "Well, don't be long packing your bags," I say.

A few patches of ice are floating on the Seine. I meet Anna for dinner with two important and rather hard-nosed investors, to win them over. We manage to get things turned around our way. It's late and I'm tired when we come out of the restaurant, and I get a text from Vincent, who's locked out of his apartment. I wait to see if Anna gets the same message. I answer that I'm on my way.

I'm pleasantly surprised that in a tight spot he reached out to me. I go pick him up and when he tells me she's changed the locks I look incensed. "That's outrageous," I say.

He's both twitchy and helpless. I think he hadn't expected such a radical reaction out of Josie and he can't get his mind around the consequences. He doesn't ask me where we're going. I drive along the river.

"I know Grandfather died," he says.

This is an area where Irène defeated me. She used Vincent's awkward years, when he would immediately take to anything that might upset or annoy his mother, to her advantage. "Don't call him Grandfather," I would say. "You don't have a grandfather. That man is nothing to you." And then I would turn to Irène and say, "When will you stop filling his head with this crap? What do you get out of it, anyway?" We had bitter arguments over it, I would literally have fits, but the position I'd taken wasn't easy to defend. I couldn't just erase a blood relation.

I glance at him, wary, but I can't make out any sarcastic intent in his use of the word "grandfather" and I'm reassured by the peaceful look on his face.

"Yes, he hanged himself," I say.

He nods and stares into space. We cross the Pont de Sèvres. "Fuck, I mean after all he was your father," he says.

When we get there, I don't need to show him where his bedroom is. He knows. I find him a toothbrush. Outside, the moon is shining in the cold night. "Seven o'clock departure tomorrow morning," I tell him. He nods, he yawns. He gives me the slightest of waves. "Thanks for helping me out, Mom," he says.

"You don't have to thank me. I'm your mother, that's what I'm here for."

"Well, thanks just the same."

He's looking around for something. I hand him a book of short stories by Eudora Welty.

"What do you think?" he asks me.

"She's one of the greatest."

"No, I mean what would you do if you were me?"

How could I have imagined he wanted my opinion? I'm in shock. I pretend to think it over, studying the pattern of the rug in the hallway outside my bedroom.

"I don't know," I say. "I don't know how much you care for her. But if I were you I wouldn't come charging back too quickly. I'd wait it out a day or two, making no contact at all. Give yourself an observation period. Make sure you master the calendar. The steadiest nerves win the day, don't forget that. And frankly, I don't know her very well but I get the feeling hers are pretty steady, that she's not the type to back down with anyone."

"Never seen anything like it. She's so impossible."

"That's what I'm saying, expect some resistance. But this isn't all bad. It'll give you both time to think about what you really want. It's a chance to test this relationship, to see if it will stand up. Because I mean, Vincent, that is something you'll have to think about at some point. Speaking of which, isn't Édouard's father supposed to get out soon?"

"I'm his father."

"Right, I understand. But what does he say about it?"

"No idea. They're separated."

"So what's the big deal about getting him out? All that money spent."

"It's about justice. The cops wanted to make an example of him. It's intolerable. Fuck."

"Right, whatever. That's just one more thing for you to consider. It's just one problem among many you're going to have to face. You must know that. There's no harm in taking everything into account. Just know I'll be there for you, whatever happens. I went through hell to bring you into the world, you understand?"

He smiles. At this rate, pretty soon he'll be hugging me every morning and every night.

I don't regret promising I'll be there for him. It's absolutely true. I'll be there for him to my dying breath, but he's in my office practically all day long, pacing up and down, gnashing his teeth behind my back, standing at my window opposite the office towers sticking up into the white, once again snowy sky, walking up and down, checking his cell, ostentatiously smoking cigarettes, while I am overloaded with work. Anna motions for me to be patient.

I have nothing for lunch and nothing that night either. "The first day is the hardest," I say.

"Really? What do you know about it?"

He picks up a shovel and in near total darkness—the moonlight isn't very hardy—he starts frantically clearing the snow outside.

When he comes back inside, he's soaked with sweat

but I can see he's gotten rid of a lot of the tension building inside him. His father used to do the same thing in winter when we had arguments. At other times he would take it out on the dead leaves, burning them, or yanking up weeds or chopping wood. I never realized Josie—though I have always been wary of the attraction weak-minded men can have for heavy-set women—I never realized Josie could leave him so distraught, that he cared about her that much. I just don't get it. I haven't been as quick, or sharp, or clever as I should have been in this whole thing. I'm nearing fifty, so that isn't exactly reassuring.

A little later, I realize once again that I'm all wrong. It's lousy mothering, but I resort to a few glasses of white wine to loosen his tongue. Be that as it may, I'm beginning to glimpse another reality taking shape little by little like a jigsaw puzzle, and the obvious fact suddenly leaps out at me: It's not Josie he wants, it's his son. It's not the woman, it's the child.

All sorts of attitudes and remarks suddenly make sense, but I couldn't see it when it was right there in front of me, couldn't hear it ringing in my ears. I wasn't capable of imagining anything beyond these never-ending couple's quarrels. I have been completely blind. I sit quietly next to him and take his hand, and he's drunk enough not to find this worrisome. I can't sleep that night. It's an enormous, dizzying, endless jumble of a night, and bright and early the next day, we run into Patrick at the minimart. Actually, Vincent and Patrick run into each other in who-knows-what aisle and come toward me together, talking and smiling like friends.

And that loathsome Patrick—wouldn't you know it?—has the gall to lean over and kiss me hello. I stiffen like I'm going to be touched by a leper, but he pays no attention, his lips landing on each cheek, even more insistently since he is holding me tightly by the biceps as he does it. When he lets go, I quickly attempt to hide my confusion, my jumpiness and flutter, grabbing the first thing I find, in this case a five-pack of number-three spaghettini, which I add to my cart and go on my way, ignoring him.

Unfortunately, he is charming this morning and, although I am as recalcitrant as I can possibly be, he winds up making me smile. Still, I avoid meeting eyes with him, in order to keep my head. Why does this have to be so complicated? Why do I wind up with a sex maniac when all I want is gentleness, calm, a little respite after all the tumultuous events of these last few months?

We're at his place, having a drink, joking, slapping together a meal on the spur of the moment. I must be hallucinating. I don't know how on earth we got here, how I could have agreed to set foot inside this house—it's a total mystery to me. It was probably Vincent in part. He thinks Patrick is a really nice guy and he's eager to get a look at that collection of five thousand vinyl LPs Patrick told us about as we came through the checkout counter and outside, under a blue sky. But I didn't merely cave in to Vincent. It's this other me coming out, though I fight it tooth and nail. It's a me that invites confusion, flux, unexplored territories. I don't know. I can't screw open my head and take a look inside. Regardless, here I am setting the table, astounded by my own fearlessness, while the boys are at work in the kitchen, clamoring for another bottle of wine. Vincent drank just the night before, but he argues that in light of the awful uncertainty in his life right now he could use a little break, a couple of laughs. He waves off my objections as he pours himself another glass. I watch him and I can feel the first signs of desertion in my ranks.

When last heard from, Rébecca spent the night somewhere near Gijón, in the Asturias region. I listen with rapt attention as Patrick goes on about his wife's pilgrimage, while Vincent sleeps with his eyes open at my side, having ignored my recommendation to go easy, thus leaving me ostensibly alone with our host who seems to want only to appear as pleasant as he can and who—however unjust this may be—succeeds with alarming ease. I know this comes from me, from my *wanting* him to succeed, and any prison screw could seem likable under those circumstances, but that's just the way it is.

It's so nice and warm here that I unbutton my sweater and ask him about his heating system.

"Wood boiler," he says, "with inverted flame combustion."

"Oh, really? Inverted flame, uh-huh."

I don't know the first thing about this, but I nod and look informed. The living room is decorated in "young white-collar"—pallid reissues and faux vintage—which gets boring very quickly, but the afternoon sun darts rays around the room, sprucing things up a little. Half asleep, Vincent slides down on the couch. His presence nevertheless changes everything and I feel fairly relaxed now that

Patrick has given me some vintage brandy to taste and it has come gunning for my last lines of defense.

"I've heard good things about ceiling heaters," I blurt.

His heating system is in the laundry room. I tell him I'm glad I got a look at all those machines, meters, electric cables, red, blue, black, and yellow pipes, the elbow joints, couplers, joiners, conduits, stopcocks, lag bolts, nuts, all that machinery. Continuing his little tour, he shows me the water heater. That's fine, too, and huge. Next to it, the highly touted boiler purrs away. I'm about to ask him if heating oil is still a viable option when he suddenly grabs my wrist. I resist. I look at him straight in the eyes. "No, not here. Not now," I tell him in a hush. He doesn't let go, backs me up against the wall, sticks his knee between my legs. I back him off with a pelvic thrust. "Vincent is upstairs," I say. He jumps me again. In our struggle, we knock over a metal cabinet and the drawers clatter onto the ground. I hit him in the face with my free hand. He roars and rubs himself against me. We go sprawling on the floor. Against a man's body, a man's strength, I don't stand a chance. But what spices it up, the thing that would make me smile if I weren't so busy fighting like a madwoman while he tries to get his penis inside me, is that it is within my power to stop this assault in one second, that it is up to me, a mere woman, whether or not to send this imbecile slinking back to his nest.

It's getting late in the afternoon but it's still nice out. I gently shake Vincent's shoulder. He has gone on with his innocent nap while, only a few steps away, I was being violated. He asks where he is, rubs his eyes and smiles, explaining that he fell asleep, though we had already gleaned as much. "It's time to go home," I say. He straightens up. Patrick brings our coats. I avoid his eyes. He sees us to the door. Vincent and I leave the house—upon closer examination, it is apparent that I am actually a step behind my son and, making use of that extra beat, I quickly turn toward Patrick and brush his lips with mine before continuing on past the car, cheeks still burning hot and cursing myself.

As evening falls, Vincent starts pacing back and forth. Now and then, passing a window, he stops and looks outside at the dusk, growing darker with every passing minute. Then he goes back to his pacing. He's very tense and nervous, the opposite of me. I'm very calmly garnishing a pizza—according to a recipe I got from Gino Sorbillo himself. I'm entirely relaxed, smooth forehead, shoulders loose, restless mood.

He finally asks me if I have any grass left because he can't take it anymore, Josie's silence has become intolerable. "Relax, they're not going anywhere," I tell him, but he isn't reassured. When we sit down to eat he feels better, but he would feel even better if that bitch—this is more often than not how he now refers to Josie—would just tell him what's going on.

I'm sorry he isn't happy. I've enjoyed these few days spent together—so different from the nightmare he and I went through after the divorce, where every day he blamed me for throwing his father out of the house, destroying our family, being merciless—and I would love to see him satisfied, like I am right now, so we can make the most of this unexpected, totally spontaneous time together.

I watch him eat the pizza I made, and for the moment that's enough to make me happy. I'm sort of floating. I'm probably still in shock—under the spell?—of this afternoon's episode, which at the same time scares me. I feel somehow ashamed. I'm well aware of all that is sick about what Patrick and I engaged in this afternoon in the laundry room, about that demented relationship, that savage encounter, but I must be honest, I must face the truth. I liked holding his body in my arms, our limbs intermingled, his penis inside me, his wet tongue, his fingers like claws digging into my burning wrists, his hands in my hair, his lips forcing me to open my mouth. I liked all of that, I *got off* on it, I *can't* pretend otherwise. I have fantasized about him so many times that I'm only half surprised, but the pure pleasure of it is such a rare prize that I'm still a little stunned, and so I only peck parsimoniously at my share of the cheese pizza.

You can't say that Vincent's powers of observation have been at their peak since we sat down, but he does start staring at me as a little smile forms on his face. "Why do you look like that?" he asks.

My eyes go wide. "I don't know. What do I look like?"

"You're somewhere else completely."

"You're the one who smoked up, Vincent. Not me."

I smile and stand up, supposedly because the salad needs spinning, in order to cut the conversation short. I feel like I've been caught with my hand in the cookie jar.

I'm glad to see that Vincent has returned to his dark brooding about being a dispossessed father and has forgotten about me. This gives me a chance to slip away for a minute and get my honest woman face back on, adjusting the clip in my hair, wiping my forehead and my slightly flush cheeks with a moist washcloth.

A little later, he really can't take it anymore and, since I'm in a good mood and I'm short on ideas, I suggest we go get a closer look at what's going on. I haven't even finished my sentence and he's already putting on his anorak.

When we get to the building, the lights are on in his apartment. We park the car. I look at Vincent. "So now what do we do? Listen, my advice is to do nothing. Look. They're in there. Everything is fine. You can relax now, right? He's her son, too. She's not going to eat him, right? Vincent, are you listening?"

No, obviously, he's not. He's leaning over, his neck craned up toward those windows. Then he says, "Do me a favor and wait for me here. Five minutes."

"No, hey, honey, this is a bad idea."

He puts his hand on mine. "It's all right," he says. "Relax. I'm just going to put my ear to the door."

"What? No, that's stupid. Don't."

"Look, I'm a grown-up."

I follow him with my eyes as he rushes through the doors of the building. I keep the motor running for the heat. This is a quiet, peaceful neighborhood on a Saturday night, but there is an icy wind blowing. This is his show, after all. His mistakes and failures will help him grow. He's almost twenty-five, I should stay out of this. He knows my opinion, whether he takes it to heart or not is up to him. I smoke a cigarette once I've opened my window an inch. I can feel I'm going to sleep very well tonight. My God. This is atrocious. I make sure I don't have any messages on my phone. I remember one man very clearly, someone I knew a few years before I met Richard, who really blew me away sexually, so much so that his memory remained painfully keen deep in my heart. Now I feel that Patrick has reactivated those forgotten sensations, which I feared I would never feel again, given that some say these are once-in-a-lifetime thrills.

My policy has been not to rush, in either direction, to keep my head. It's clear that the problem has no solution. Having kissed Patrick on the lips is not going to make things any simpler, I'm well aware of that. I am pondering with regret that stupid adolescent kiss I bestowed upon him on my way out, as if the rest were not enough, and at that instant I see Vincent bursting through the lobby and racing to the car with the newborn in his arms. He jumps into the backseat. "Drive!" he barks. "Fucking drive!"

I drive for a good minute without a word, then I pull over and turn around to Vincent to ask him if he's completely out of his mind. I start to explain what kind of trouble he's in but Édouard abruptly starts screaming his head off, making communication impossible and splitting our eardrums for a while.

Then Vincent manages to calm him down. I watch him in the rearview mirror and he seems rather good at it, rather self-assured.

"Is there any milk at home?" he asks.

"You think I might have infant formula in my cupboard? That I have an assortment of diapers on hand? Vincent, you're going to give this child back to his mother. You understand?"

He's not foolish enough to think he can pull this off, knows he acted too impulsively. But I think in the end he has what he wanted. He has taken Édouard upstairs for a bath and I am bowled over by his attentions with this baby, by the tenderness he shows him. I have never imagined Vincent in this light and he is also showing Josie that he is willing to fight, that there are no limits to what he'll do. He's killed two birds with one stone. That's a good thing. I warm up in front of the fire and I call Josie to explain the situation to her.

Right off the bat, she spares me no part of her bad mood. If I am hearing correctly, Vincent's exploit caused a bit of a stir inside the apartment and now her compact stereo is in pieces.

"Don't worry about your stereo, Josie, I'll take care of that. Concerning your child, he's safe, you know that. You can come get him when you like, Josie. Come tomorrow if it's convenient. Vincent is aware that his act was over the line. But apart from that, is everything all right? Nothing else was broken? I can hear them laughing right upstairs. Vincent is giving him a bath. Really, what a terrible fuss!"

"Well, you were the one driving the car."

"Excuse me? I was driving the car? What? Well, yeah, I guess I was at the wheel, but what would you have me do? I'm his mother, Josie. You'll see, very soon, exactly what that means. But all's well that ends well, right? I was driving, but I was shivering in fright, you know. Are you mad at me? Come on now, let's put this whole thing behind us. You like movies. I'm going to get you a subscription to the movie channels, all right?"

"I like animals and history, too. And the human body."

I can never tell if this girl has a ferocious sense of humor or if it's just the opposite, no sense of humor at all. I sigh with relief when I hang up and immediately pour myself a drink. I have had enough emotion for one day, and as if by magic, snow starts to fall once again and the house is wrapped and muffled in its alb.

I smoke near the window, listening to Dustin O'Halloran's "We Move Lightly," then I go up to join them. Édouard is wriggling around on the bed, a terry cloth towel around him. "I found some talcum powder," Vincent says. I nod, leaning against the doorjamb. I usually never enter his bedroom—not for sentimental reasons but because the only reason I have to go inside is to air it out. The picture of the two of them here together in this setting pretty much makes my head spin.

"Josie will stop by tomorrow," I say.

He doesn't answer. In the attic I find the carriage that was his, and that vindicates Richard who had decided to keep it even though all I wanted was to get rid of it once and for all, burn it if we had to, just to make sure I never had to go through that experience again. "Maybe he doesn't have much to eat or wear," I remark as I extract the contraption from its cover, "but now he's got a bed."

Vincent joins me once the baby's asleep. "I traveled miles and miles with you in that thing," I say. "It has wonderful suspension." As he is less interested in my youthful memories than in Josie's reaction, I endeavor to relate our conversation as faithfully as I can. He thinks it over a moment, then calls Anna to clear up a few legal points, while I squeeze lemons and whip up some hot toddies. Through the kitchen window, I can see lights on at Patrick's. Nothing more than a flickering glow behind a curtain of snow, but I refuse to think about it.

Totally impossible. Not thinking about it is totally impossible. Experience, reason, intelligence, age are of no assistance. I am ashamed of it, I am slain. At this rate, what will be left of my pride? Vincent has stepped out to get some firewood and an icy draft comes through the room at the very moment I ask myself that question, and it chills me to the bone.

I'm sorry I'm not a believer, I'd go see a priest. Faith is still the best remedy in the world. I think a good old-fashioned confession would soothe me. I would love to be convinced that God sees me.

We're speaking of just how fragile love relationships are and how couples most often fly apart—and with time, Vincent concedes that the blame was shared between his father and me—when Anna arrives to join the party and, taking off her coat, announces that it's all over between her and Robert, who in the end has always been a pig.

"Wait, what are you talking about?" I ask, a little worried.

"He's having an affair," she says. "Really, can you imagine?"

She kisses us hello. It's a good thing there's a fire—you can't see I've gone white.

She takes Vincent's hands in hers. "Poor darling," she says. "Our love lives aren't going very well right now."

"Have a sip of my toddy," he says.

"Robert? An affair?" I ask weakly.

"And get this, it's been going on for years."

"Fuck, that sucks," offers Vincent.

"What do you say to that?" Anna asks me.

"Listen, I'm flabbergasted."

"I couldn't get over it either. I had to sit down."

"Of course," says Vincent in sympathy.

I get up to poke the logs and straighten out the fire. No one ever thought that she and Robert had the perfect marriage and that they loved each other deeply, but she doesn't seem too terribly upset by his betrayal.

"I'm not saying it doesn't affect me," she says to underscore the nuance, "but it's not affecting me that much. Since yesterday, it's like there's this stranger walking around the place. You can just imagine how good that feels. A man I don't recognize at all."

I nod. I turn around and go make more toddies. When I come back, Vincent has just finished jotting down the address of a lawyer. The snow is falling, the fire is crackling. He goes upstairs to make sure the baby is fast asleep while I do the pouring.

"I should be glad he didn't give me a disease or something," she says with a sigh.

"Are you hungry?" I ask. "Have you eaten?"

I relax a little when I learn that she has no idea who the woman is and isn't interested in finding out. "I don't know," I say, "but maybe in the end you're right. I'm really sorry, you know?"

"You don't need to be sorry. I'm fine. Life is full of incidents like this."

I raise one arm and she comes over and nestles at my

shoulder. A few minutes later, when Vincent comes downstairs and sees this, he smiles a little. Anna raises her arm and he nestles at her shoulder. We don't speak. We look toward the fire. Then I leave them, I go up to bed.

At times I have wondered, when he wasn't quite old enough to shave and then again later on, if certain things happened between them. But I have never been sure about it and this morning does nothing to change that. I don't know if they slept together or if she slept on the couch and I guess I never will know because no matter how closely I watch, hoping they will tip their hand one way or the other, I notice nothing out of the ordinary, only the little affectionate gestures they have exchanged since he was born, which don't tell me anything I don't already know.

Vincent goes out to buy what he needs for the baby and when I come back downstairs Anna is clutching him to her breast like a fragile treasure, leaning her face toward him and dancing him around so easy and lithe, so tenderly and affectionately, you would swear she was at the very least his mother. But knowing the tragedy she lived through twice, the frustration like an open wound that never heals and only deepens, I keep my distance, not getting involved, and when Vincent gets back and they think they're alone, I watch their eyes, watch for the slightest brush of a hand, the detail that might give them away, but they are exceedingly good at this. It's practically laughable.

What does turn out to be ludicrous, however, is the duo they form, hovering over Édouard as if they were his parents, a couple of head cases teaming up. I say I'm going out for a while, but I'm not going anywhere.

It's a nice day, the snow creaks and cracks under my rubber boots. Taking a walk is the best thing in the world. When I get to Patrick's, he's out in the garden, in shirtsleeves, clearing the snow. When he sees me, he stops and motions to me, friendly as you please. "Hello, how are you?" he calls out with a big smile.

"Fine. And you?"

He leans his elbow on his shovel and looks up to the sky, still smiling. "I'm all inside out," he finally says.

"Really?" I ask warily. "You would go that far? Inside out?"

I am thinking, nodding my head. "We're going to have to talk, Patrick."

"I know, of course," he says, bowing his head.

"We're going to have to talk very soon, you know. You've given me a big problem, Patrick." We look at each other intensely for a moment, then I break it off by briskly turning around. I walk away a few steps, then I stop and turn back toward him. "Just so you know, I am, too. I'm inside out, as you put it." With that, I start walking again, catching my breath as I go along.

Josie refuses to have coffee with us, even though I've relegated Anna to my office so they won't run into each other and I've opened an excellent box of chocolates and left it out on the table. She explains that she was very angry and that only my quick phone call to let her know what was going on prevented a report to the authorities for kidnapping, breaking and entering, assault, and who knows what else. But that doesn't mean she's going to sit down and have a pleasant chat about what happened. I understand completely. This speaks well for her, but I can't tell her that.

"Think of him, both of you," I say. "Think less about yourselves and more about him. Be smart. Try to find some common ground."

She sniggers. "Should've tried that sooner."

"Okay, okay," says Vincent with a sigh.

"Not what I call an apology."

There is apparently a problem with the zipper on the fluorescent green snowsuit that we've stuffed him into and that immediately turned him into a little butterball—though the mother is herself a two-hundred-pound woman wrapped in a horrid silvery-turquoise down coat, so a certain balance has been struck.

I try to reason with her. "Let him accept this job," I say. "This is no time to be messing around with that. There's a season for this and a season for that. You know it, Josie."

"Stay out of it," she says.

"Stay out of it," says Vincent.

I don't say a word. I give a good, firm tug on the zipper and it comes unstuck.

We watch her leave. "She's not as inflexible as all that," I say. "Time is on your side. In three days, she'll be on her knees."

"No, don't bet on that," he says, while she disappears around the first curve and into the bluish woods. "She's surprised me more than once. She might surprise me again."

Anna stays for a while after Josie leaves. I'm sure she heard everything but she pretends she hasn't, cocking her head and listening carefully to Vincent's version, trying to take the temperature of things. Anna is an expert. Josie is a delicate piece to handle if you're not very aware of Vincent's feelings for her. But is he himself aware? That's the heart of the problem, his dogged and perhaps unconscious uncertainty, that's what makes this so difficult, and Anna does well to get herself up to speed because it appears that Josie's stock is not quite as low in Vincent's esteem as we thought it was, that he's not quite as indifferent as he says he is, that we might just find ourselves in an awkward position as soon as the wind turns if we don't get constant updates.

On her way out, I see her to the door and she's pulling her gloves on when she whispers, without looking at me, "Get ready for pain."

"What does that mean?" I ask.

"It means get ready for pain."

She kisses me goodbye and she's off, leaving me with this riddle.

The next day at the office, I get a moment alone with her and I ask her to explain. I say, "I thought a lot about what you said on your way out yesterday."

"She's going to hurt us. I can feel it. But there's no way to avoid it. She's going to wind up hurting us, I know it."

We smoke a cigarette. "Starting a week with gloomy thoughts like that. It's so depressing."

"Yes, I know. What can I say?" She sighs. "It's like a revelation. I can just feel it coming."

I watch Vincent as he comes over to the coffee machine. I watch him eating at lunchtime. I watch him at closing time. But I don't know what I'm looking for.

In any case, I'm thinking about asking him if he's planning on staying at the house for any length of time. I'm afraid he'll take it wrong, but his presence does make certain things a little complicated—like having a secret liaison, for example.

I was thrilled that Josie threw him out and I have thoroughly enjoyed his company these past few days, enjoying every minute he spent at the house with me, liked him eating there, washing there, sleeping there, calling to me from down the hall, roaming around in his bathrobe, thundering down the stairs, clearing the snow out front, not being just a visitor—and I was happy he was here for a host of other reasons, but then there was the incident in the laundry room and since then I've been wanting to lead my life as I see fit, far from prying eyes. In short, I would rather he weren't here but here he is, he's underfoot now, and I can't see Patrick again for three days—Josie finally allowed Vincent to babysit two evenings a week.

Evening. I drink a tall glass of gin and I tell him to come over. I show him in and tell him to pour himself a drink. I feel a little on edge. This isn't such a simple matter.

"This isn't such a simple matter," I tell him. "When you think about it, you're nothing but a disgusting little rapist, you raped me. Do you realize what you did to me? Do you think I can forgive you for that?" He sits down and buries his face in his hands.

"Oh, no, don't you dare!" I say to him, very annoyed. I light a cigarette.

I start pacing up and down and he looks up. I pick up my coat. "Let's go outside," I say. "Let's get some air."

It's very cold, the moonlight is welcoming. We don't go far, we stay right outside, standing side by side in the night air. "The air really smells good, don't you think? Say something. Aren't you cold?"

"No, I'm not."

"Are you sure? You're only wearing a shirt."

"No, I'm not."

"Can you put yourself in my shoes?"

I don't look at him, but the fog from his breath enters my field of vision. "What am I supposed to do with you?" I ask. "Help me out, tell me what I'm supposed to do."

I sneak a peek at him and I can tell he doesn't know any better than I do. I can see he's trying to figure it out, too, that he would like to understand better, but it's hopeless.

"I can't do anything otherwise," he says after a moment.

"I got that," I say. "I'm not blind."

Then he belabors the point, loud and clear: "I can't get it up otherwise, you understand?"

Now I look right at him, then I shrug and look elsewhere. "This is insane," I say with a sigh.

I keep looking at the sky for another minute or two, then I suggest we go back inside and get warm.

I have to wait two more days to see him again, wait until Vincent has another evening with Édouard so I'm free and we do it again. We have a drink to kick-start things, then he promptly jumps me and we are quickly rolling around on the floor, our savage battle begun. He tears off my clothes and I scream. I punch him, for real, with my fists. He puts his hands around my throat, hits me, possesses me, and so forth.

Over the weekend, I buy a batch of cut-rate lingerie.

After thinking it over, we decided to throw that AV Productions twenty-fifth anniversary party and Vincent is taken away from his not-too-strenuous archiving work and given a much tougher, time-consuming task—which leaves me suddenly and magically free for a few evenings because he's knocking himself out all day long, running all over the place, from the printers to the suppliers, solving a mountain of small problems that never seem to end, never losing his cool. And so he's falling asleep in the car on the way home and he goes straight upstairs to his bedroom and his evening is over while mine, so to speak, has just begun.

I lie down and read for a while—I don't like all of David Foster Wallace, but it's often fantastic—while I wait for him to fall asleep. I go past his door to make sure. If there is no ray of light coming from underneath, no sound from within for a minute or so, I tiptoe away and go outside.

I cross through the garden to the curb, cross the road, stroll out in the open, past the few bushes heavy with snow sparkling in the moonlight, hands in pockets, alone, hearing a bird call, smiling because the idea that Vincent might wake up and realize I'm gone is almost sweet as candy. Then I go up to the house with the lighted windows and the smoke rising from the chimney.

Patrick thinks that when we're in the cellar, I can scream my head off all I want and we'll never wake the neighbors. That's reassuring to me because I have no idea how I would explain screaming like I was going to have my throat cut, or how on earth I could be playing such idiotic and perverse games at my age.

I haven't taken the time to think about it. I don't have a minute to myself, and when I miraculously manage to see Patrick we're much too busy with our deviant encounters to take stock of what we're doing and I put off really thinking about it. Probably out of fear that it might be indefensible—I can't count that out.

No one could possibly believe that I don't get pleasure out of these terrifying charades, as twisted as they are—but I never denied it, I never said it was platonic. I feel like I've awakened from a long slumber and I realize just how much being with Robert had become a tiresome and indifferent affair toward the end.

I'm aware that things cannot remain this way forever, that we're going to have to talk about this soon, but there is also the fear that if we do talk it could all vanish in a single breath, and that fear is petrifying. When I begin to retrace my steps on the way home, happy, aching and sore, having practically lost my voice, he offers to see me to my door. But I would rather leave as I arrived, on foot, using the cold of the night to bring my body and my mind back to normal temperature.

One evening, after an arduous day, Vincent tells me that things with Josie aren't getting any better and that he's thinking about going to court if he can't obtain a more equitable arrangement for custody of Édouard.

"For example," he explains, "I could take him in the evening when I get out of work, then bring him back the next morning on my way in. I could feed him at night, wash him, put him to bed, then change him the next morning, comb his hair, give him breakfast."

I merely nod. What good would it do to point out the enormity and the absurdity of the task he's about to take on? Is there the slightest chance he'll listen to reason? We go for a drink before we go home. Anna joins us. This party is making her anxious, and Robert, who's supposed to be staying at a hotel while things are up in the air, is constantly prowling around the apartment looking for a necktie or a pair of shoes he couldn't take with him. "It's exhausting," she says with a sigh. "I guess he's doing it on purpose."

When Vincent goes downstairs to the men's room, I ask Anna not to encourage this crazy idea of Vincent's that could land us with a newborn baby to take care of, not all day long but all night long, which is the worst bit. "Can you imagine, after a day like this, having to play nursemaid to an infant? Think about it, please. I don't want that."

"What do you want?"

"I have no idea. All I know is, I don't want that. I want to be able to go home and run myself a bath, nothing else."

"But this is important to him."

"I felt we had found a nice balance. Every other day is enough for me. Don't ask me for more. Don't bother. I need to have a couple of nights free, you understand? You have to keep a little space for yourself, you know that. That's important, too."

"Listen, they could stay with me a couple of nights a week. I don't know, what do you think?"

"I think he isn't going to make it. I think letting him believe he will is not helping him."

"We're going to help him. We can make it work."

I don't say anything. I drink my gin and tonic through a straw.

That evening, I scream with every ounce of strength, I call for help and thrash around like a wild animal and, in the end, Patrick rolls over on his side, sweating, out of breath, then lies there with his arms crossed and smiling up at the ceiling. He gives me a little whistle, as if to tell me that I played my role brilliantly, exceptionally well. I can see his nose is bleeding a little. Then he hoists himself up on one elbow and gazes at me, enthralled.

Vincent does a good job of it, renting a houseboat near the Mitterrand Library, hiring a British DJ, and negotiating the rest with Chez Flo, getting each item at the best possible price. Everyone at the company thinks he's great. He's helpful, committed to his assignment, and we're starting to think that hiring him is justified by more than an act of charity—well, I'm starting to think so, Anna says she never doubted it. But naturally there's something wrong. His problems with Josie cast a shadow over everything, taking all the pleasure out of it. I have time to listen to him at length on the way home, so I know they are far from any agreement and things are getting hairy. In one sense that's reassuring for me, because I see that my fears have been premature, but in another sense it's worrisome, catching a glimpse of his dark expression by the greenish glow of the dashboard lights.

I have always feared that my father passed something along to me, that I am nothing more than a cursed link in a cursed chain.

"Tell her I want to see her, tell her I want to talk to her."

I swerve to avoid a cyclist teetering on a municipal bike rental.

"Watch where you're going," he says after jumping out of his seat. "You're driving a fucking car."

He drinks too much coffee.

"You're always so wound up," I say.

The day before the party, he's still out running around, checking that everything's been checked, that the cake will be ready, making sure there is no snowfall or transportation strike looming that might disrupt the evening. Then he calls Josie and I get the feeling they have started to quibble over scheduling issues and he walks away because the exchange is getting hotter, peppered with angry flashes, and soon all I can make out is the ordinary and predictable litany that is now their poor excuse for conversation, and then he vanishes down the emergency staircase, as if leaving a trail of flame in his wake.

He hasn't slept a wink, he tells me. He took two Valiums, which had absolutely no effect on him, then he played solitaire for hours on his phone, finally stopping at sunrise. "I brought some firewood in," he adds.

I touch his cheek tenderly. I yawn. I went to see Patrick at about midnight and I could use a few more hours of sleep, but I have no regrets.

"What's going to happen when Rébecca gets back?" I asked him.

He brushed away a lock of hair matted with sweat to my forehead and, smiling, answered that he'll probably get a hotel room for a while. "Like our friend Robert," he added, laughing—though I'm the only one who can truly appreciate the irony of the remark. He says Rébecca is going to stop in Lourdes on her way back and wonders—only half joking—if she might take a detour through Jerusalem or Bugarach or something. I'm sort of on a cloud—or rather *inside* a cloud—and so nothing can really hit me, at best things sort of kiss up against me. We did it in his garage this time, on the hood of his car, and I know that doesn't help me to get my feet back on the ground, but this won't—can't—go on. We're going to have to clear this whole thing up, very soon. In the next few days.

Vincent made breakfast. "Great. Thank you, Vincent. But now sit down and don't do anything else. Rest. Unwind."

"I've got the jitters. I busted my ass, you know what I mean?"

"You can relax. People will come. There will be food and drink. It will all go fine."

"I couldn't get through to her all night, she didn't answer."

"Of course not, Vincent. She sleeps at night. Normal people do that, you know?"

He has gotten the eggs ready, I need only cook them.

"Look, Vincent, I don't think this is the right way about it, you know? Harassing her. I see her as the type who will answer every blow a hundred times over."

He grumbles unintelligibly. I feel sorry for him. I would be so glad if he would forget all about Josie and her child, if he just let them go on with a life they embarked upon without him—jumping on board a moving vehicle is always hard and implies some acrobatic efforts. All he would need to do is let go, just go out and get good and drunk and it would all be over. But I steadfastly avoid giving him my opinion. I don't want to take any risks, only hours away from a party that already has him tied up in knots.

No one knows about my affair with Patrick, but he is

now in our circle of acquaintances and on our guest list. He's going to give me a lift because I'm letting Vincent have the car. Really starting to get worried, he wants to go take a look for himself.

Vincent has only just left when Patrick shows up and we can hear the motor purring. He looks at me, smiling. I quickly let him know what's going on and I can see his expression change. Now I smile. "Don't even think about it," I tell him. "Don't force me to pepper-spray you."

"You're tempting me, Michèle."

I touch his arm. "We won't come home late," I say, shamelessly squeezing his arm. "I promise you," I add, staring him right in the eyes and pouting.

"You're torturing me," he says breathily, close to my neck.

"I certainly hope so, Patrick."

I had forgotten how good it is to have a new lover, how every instant together is filled with surprise, freshness, explosiveness, at least for the first three weeks. How good it feels to play around, to hide, to keep a secret, to joke. He tells me I'm fabulous as we walk out into the cold night. *Now that's what I like to hear*, I think to myself, *that's the most powerful drug in the world.*

Blocks of ice come floating and shimmering along the Seine and slide up against the black hull of the houseboat.

Richard isn't up to speed on the persistent difficulties between Josie and his son, which gives me a chance to tell him he must learn to better manage his time, instead of giving nine-tenths of it to Hélène, if he hopes to still have a clue about the world around him. He lets out a nervous laugh. I heard that Hélène got Hexagone to read his screenplay—something I have always failed to do, he must have immediately thought—and I imagine that the remaining tenth has been spent burning candles for her. "In any event, he hasn't heard a peep from her since yesterday. Not a good sign. Give him some attention. Talk to him."

He hands me a glass of champagne and nods. The houseboat pitches slightly as a horrid *bateau-mouche* goes by. Usually, he would respond by saying I'm one to talk or something along those lines. That combative mind-set he used to have with me is starting to disappear just as the snow will start to melt on the first warm days. The paradox is, this lack of hostility is hurtful. Richard and I have had time to say three words together and already there are three men talking to her and he is keeping watch out of the corner of his eye and frowning weakly.

Anna joins me at the bar. She wants to compliment Vincent because everything is going so smoothly, but she can't find him. She knits her eyebrows when I tell her why he isn't there. She says nothing. She clenches her fists. I don't point it out, but this unabashed dislike of Josie—though it's quite mutual—is at the root of the conflict between Josie and Vincent, and this is what happens. But I take her in my arms because this party is thanks to her. Twenty-five years ago we met in a hospital room and we started all this going and I hold her close for a minute, until some start to whistle and call out in encouragement.

Anna rides the mood, speaking of her emotion, her pride, thanking all of AV Productions' friends and partners from the bottom of her heart—they have been at our side throughout these twenty-five years and blah blah blah, then everyone applauds. A few writers are drunk. The champagne is excellent. Vincent has indeed done a fine job. I wonder what he's up to. I make sure some petits fours are put aside for him. Now and then, I run into Patrick and we exchange a few banalities, as any passing acquaintances might, and this turns out to be fairly amusing because we are thinking of only one thing—our next encounter—and feigning indifference under those circumstances takes on an uncommon flavor. So much so that Anna whispers in my ear, speaking of Patrick, that she still can't fathom how I haven't fallen for my charming neighbor. I look at him out of the corner of my eye. "Don't you think he's a little bland? Sort of ordinary?" I ask.

Vincent finally shows up, but he's alone. And he is white as a ghost. Generous and charitable, I go out and meet him on the dock. "She's not there. There's nobody home. She fucking split!"

I take his arm as we turn back toward the gangway. "No way. Are you sure?"

"I waited an hour. Then the guy downstairs told me he saw her leaving, with a suitcase."

"Is that all?"

"What? Isn't that enough?"

I lead him inside so he can admire his work, so he can feel gratified about having pulled the whole thing off without a hitch, start to finish. Anna comes over and leads him away. I give Richard the news. "Where does he think she's going with a suitcase and a baby in her arms?" he wonders, shrugging his shoulders. "She can't have gotten very far." I agree with him, and I wouldn't worry anymore about what happened to Josie if only Vincent would relax a little and lose that frown he's been wearing since he got here, unwaveringly constant. I ask Richard to go reassure him if he can, as they say only a father can, and I see in his eyes as he darts a sorry look at Hélène, still very much the center of attention in her bright red spike heels, that he feels like a guy who parked his Aston Martin in the dead of night on a block where you wouldn't leave your bicycle or your beat-up old scooter.

He finally nods.

"You're a good father," I tell him.

He keeps nodding, lost in thought.

"Richard," I say, "if she is going to get swept away the first time you have your back turned, then I advise you to get rid of her quickly. You'll only make yourself bitter and disappointed." He's one of a new race of men, with whom we have lived and live no longer, and who against all expectations remain endearing in a certain light and in moderate doses.

The cake is the size of a Ping-Pong table, thick as a brick, with a white and blue cream marbled icing, topped by a nougatine figure honoring AV Productions' twenty-fifth anniversary. I let Anna preside after blowing out the candles and playing diva to the laudatory applause and whistles from our fellow professionals. She takes legitimate pleasure in it and has a word or two in confidence with certain guests as she hands them their cake. I give her a wink and she returns it with a big smile. I see Richard thread his way through the armchairs and over to Vincent, then put a hand on his shoulder. I find Patrick at the bar—this particular Patrick is a mixture of them both, a rather unfortunate overlapping of his two faces, which makes him at once attractive and repulsive, and not far from resembling my father. I make good and sure I don't get too close to him. "Everything okay?" I ask. "You're not bored?"

It seems he has run into some acquaintances and invites me to come have a drink with them. I can see from a distance which people he's talking about—a horrible Frenchwoman who has a gallery in Soho—and I immediately bow out, saying Vincent and I have to work something out quickly, regarding the car. For a second he looks hurt but he quickly pulls it together. To congratulate him, I secretly brush his hand.

I am glad to see some old acquaintances again, in particular one couple who worked with us on portraits of artists and who came with their eighteen-year-old daughter, Aliette, who I never knew existed and who is seven and a half months pregnant, radiant, beaming, even though, if I understood correctly, the father is nowhere to be found. I also have a couple of drinks with some writers who have a wonderful story—I listen to them, smiling, not understanding a word because of the general noise level, the laughter, the voices calling out, the background music. Anna and I take a walk through the coffee tables, exchanging a few words with this person and that, as the night wears on, and I have a great evening on this houseboat. Everyone does. We all have an excellent evening on this houseboat, still on the water, except for my son. Who has just received an awful message. It's getting pretty late and I don't understand why that girl isn't sleeping at one in the morning when it's hardly been a day since I held her out as an example. I mean, doesn't she have anything better to do than to fire bullets directly at Vincent with her goddamn text messages?

"Don't try to reach me." The message is clear. I hand him back his phone. I look him straight in the eyes, but he lowers his head.

"If she sees you're trying to hang on, you're through," I tell him. I sit there next to him for a second, stroke his back, then I get up because I have come to the conclusion that there's nothing better I can do.

Later, when I think he's in the bathroom—Josie's disappearance might well make him sick to his stomach, he has implied—he calls me to say he is staking out his apartment and he would like to keep the car. "She has to come by at some point," he says, "and when she does, I'll be here."

"Look, Vincent, I don't know. You might be right. Well, I mean it's absolutely freezing out tonight, don't catch cold. But you know, one day you'll have to explain to me why you have to make things so complicated."

"Uh-huh."

"I'm serious."

One hour later, the party is still going great guns but I'm ready to go home and I can guess by the look of impatience in Patrick's eyes that I'm not the only one. I rush through it as quickly as I can, but I can't just walk out, I can't afford to be impolite with the five or six influential people whom Anna and I must pamper like rare treasures, lest we forfeit their indispensable support. You can't win if you don't play, right?

The delay has upset Patrick and he is already waiting in his car when I get outside. Richard detained me a good ten minutes more so I could give him the lowdown on the latest twists in the story and he tells me he spent an hour explaining to Vincent that he was better off doing nothing and waiting for Josie to make the first move because, as he may have noticed, she's not exactly easygoing and she might not like being boxed into a corner.

"I didn't take too long, did I?" I ask, as Patrick drives away without a word. Another little boy, I think to myself, though the physical differences are instantly apparent.

I take a good look at his profile, his lips. "Are you the brooding type, Patrick?"

I'm slightly drunk, but not drunk enough to get into an argument with him. I haven't forgotten the promise I made earlier and the very thought of it conjures a dark desire in me. With anyone else, it might be easy to make things better with a kiss or a caress, but Patrick is different. There's nothing I can do for him unless it's staged the way he likes it.

I don't want to think about that right now. I'm so ashamed that I sometimes wake up, breathless, and my thoughts just freeze when I try to imagine an acceptable resolution to an affair that has been so demeaning. A sigh rises in my breast but I keep silent. I would like it to be like some disease I caught, germs I picked up because I didn't wash my hands thoroughly, some virus for which I had no defenses, but I can't quite bring it off, I can't quite convince myself.

"Yeah, well, you certainly ditched me," he finally blurts

as we drive past the miserable abandoned buildings that were once the Samaritaine department store.

"Oh, I did not, of course not," I say, "but I do have certain obligations, certain duties. You understand that, don't you? Anyway, it wasn't you, it was that woman, that gallery owner from Soho. I happen to know her, you see. I can't stand her, I avoid her. Whatever. She's going to bust the buttons on that fuchsia suit soon, don't you think?"

A little later, he suggests we stop and do it in the woods because he can't stand to wait any longer. He wipes his mouth with the back of his hand. But I immediately burst his balloon when I tell him the temperature outside. "I'm just as impatient as you, Patrick. But not here." He gives me a predatory grin and guns the engine.

He's very excited. A little before we arrive, he leans over and opens the glove compartment, removing his ski mask, which he has the good taste to stick in my face. I raise my eyes to heaven and he lets go a sardonic laugh. Dawn seems to shimmer on the horizon. He's so excited in fact that he reaches over to caress my hair and suddenly grabs it to have me at his mercy, and veers wildly around a curve. We finally get to the house. The living room windowpanes still glow a dim red from the remaining embers in the fireplace.

Seeing us come in, Marty withdraws upstairs—my screaming frightens him.

I know that screaming is convincing. It expresses the very real rage that wells from deep inside me, drowns me, overwhelms me like some conquering army, yet I know that it also springs from the terrible pleasure I get when I'm with him.

I'm ashamed to play this game, but shame is not a strong enough sentiment to prevent anything at all.

I ask him if he wants a drink before we get into our roles, adding that I for one could do with a little foreplay for a change, but he doesn't bother to answer, thumps me good, sends me sprawling on the floor.

I hadn't expected it and it is the surprise that stuns me more than the blow itself. I kick out and send a chair flying into his feet while he slips his ski mask on. He jumps out of the way and the man now standing over me is nothing less than the devil incarnate. He rips my dress. I scream. He tries to grab my hands or my feet. I push him away. He catches me. I scream. He falls on top of me. I get my teeth into his arm. He breaks away and tries to get his penis between my legs, struggling like mad, and when he finally manages, when I'm wet and screaming louder and louder, I see Vincent standing behind him and I hear Patrick's skull crack under the pressure of the log with which my son has just sent him to meet his maker before I could say boo.

I AM THE ONLY ONE WHO KNOWS THE TRUTH. I'm the only one who knows that scene was staged and I will carry the secret to my grave. For Vincent, it's infinitely better that way. If he ever learned that he killed a man who was only engaging in the same perverse sex play as his own mother, his currently positive attitude toward me would take a hit. I'm sure of it. I water the flowers in the garden with my mind at ease on that score. They're thirsty. We have had some very warm days. It's only mid-June and it feels like midsummer already and even at this hour with the cool water from the hose the setting sun burns my cheeks.

Soon the bees will all be gone—despite the promise I made to Irène at her grave—but I can spot a few buzzing around my hydrangeas and I glance at the mosquito netting covering Édouard. He's still asleep and Vincent and Josie have gone for a walk in the woods in the meantime.

I put some cream on my arms and legs. I was watching Josie do just that a few minutes ago and I was once again struck by what a transformation she has undergone in only a few months. She is another woman, plain and simple.

She is accommodating with me, though to say I am wary of her would be a gross understatement—and that, at least, is one thing that Anna and I still share. I think Josie hates us all, actually, because we didn't welcome her with open arms and her freshly minted beauty is above all a demonstration of her power.

The house where Patrick and Rébecca lived is shown twice in the afternoon and I watch as the agency manager closes the shutters before she leaves. She is having trouble selling it—"People *know*! That poor young woman, it's awful." And for an instant I think she's speaking of me.

I smoke a cigarette, making sure that the smoke doesn't take a sudden unfortunate detour over the baby carriage. When he wakes up and starts whining, I stick one foot over the side of my deck chair and rock him gently with my toes, while I go on reading a short story by John Cheever—only an earthquake could tear me away from it.

On their way out, when he's kissing me goodbye, Vincent mentions that he's found a job at the QuickBurger and I congratulate him.

I pick up Marty and watch them go.

I stay alone through the weekend.

I'm weary. I haven't gotten over this thing; it has affected me more deeply than I allowed and, any way I look at it, leaves me torn and wounded. Following that tragic event, I dedicated every ounce of energy I had to Vincent. I remember that the first thing I did, wearing nothing but a blouse torn to shreds and panty hose rolled up in a ball at my ankle, was to unceremoniously shove him into the kitchen to shield him from the terrifying spectacle of the body in convulsion, the skull smashed, blood oozing through the ski mask like cream through a sieve. I hardly took any time for myself, and getting my head back together was not an easy task. I must have a magnesium deficiency—and a lot of other deficiencies, truth be told.

I don't want to talk about it. I have been missing Irène. Bad time for this falling-out with Anna, but Robert had become too insistent so I had no choice but to tell her what had been going on behind her back. Well, whatever else you say, I no longer have my friend, I no longer have a number I can dial when things go wrong, or when they go right, for that matter, so that when I reach for my phone I wind up grabbing my lemonade, while Marty painstakingly jumps onto my lap—it looks to me like his paw hurts—and turns around on my belly before settling down, getting a half smile out of me because he doesn't usually take these liberties. But hey, I'm open to change.

Richard apparently got into a fight with Robert in a bar a few days after my confession. I didn't want the details. And, though there is no correlation, things are better now between Richard and me—he's single again, so that probably has something to do with it—but I can't find a good reason to call him right now, so I don't. I remain alone, listening to the wind in the trees, the birds, feeling the daylight fade behind the thin veil of my closed eyelids. I know he, too, is having a hard time getting over the fact that Robert and I slept together for years and I know he's hoping to get something out of it, to get me to give up on some of the things I blame him for, especially his slapping me, but I'm afraid that may not be possible.

Just yesterday, we once again had a squabble about that. According to him, I am frightfully stubborn and hard, not to say cruel, and it's downright scary. The exchange got fairly testy when he made a remark about my refusal to grant my father one final visit—a perfect example of my outrageous inflexibility—but I couldn't listen to him judge my behavior regarding an old man who was rotting in prison, so I put earbuds in and started listening to Peter Broderick's "Everything I Know" while watching his muted lips move and I waited for him to talk himself out and, being ill-tempered by nature, refused his invitation to have dinner in town. Even now, he just doesn't understand that you can't always make a separate peace, that there is a line that must never be crossed, that there is such a thing as damnation.

The ordeal I went through over the winter gives him cause to go easy on me, as much as possible, not to upset me too much, but if he knew what was really going on, if he knew what a horrendous act I had actually been playing at, if he knew just how different things were from what they appeared, then I wager that he—and everyone else, for that matter, not to speak of Vincent—would change their view of things.

The very thought of it makes my throat close up a little and so makes it hard to breathe.

My share of the blame is enormous. I thank heaven that Patrick really did rape me, at least once, or else the guilt would have driven me mad, and I have held on to that thin thread up until now, that one thought, that he had paid for a sin that he *nevertheless did* commit. Well, I couldn't say if this was enough, but it was all I had and it was a real nightmare, a curse. Marty purrs softly on my belly. The weather is fair as evening settles. I can hear barking in the distance. I'll go in soon.

Looking back, I don't quite understand how I could ever have played such a horrendous game—unless the sex explains everything, but I'm not really sure. When you get right down to it, I never thought of myself as such a strange person, so complicated, at once so strong and so weak. It's astonishing. The experience of solitude and passing time is astonishing. The experience of oneself. Bolder women than I have wavered—though I did more than waver, to be sure. At times I see our encounters again, watch them for some reason, as if floating a few feet above those two wild beasts waging battle on the floor below, and I am blown away by my performance, by my fury, my screams of sheer terror—which apparently prevented us from hearing Vincent come in and which convinced him that at the very least I was going to get my throat slit—and nearly moved to tears as I buckle under the sustained assault, trembling like a waif from having come too much or too hard. So strong and so weak.

When I stand up, Marty falls to the ground. He's an old cat with slowing reflexes and I wasn't looking out for him. I tell him I'm sorry and lead him to the kitchen where I cut him a piece of melon. I see him stagger into the room, obviously still half asleep. He had run off after the tragedy and I didn't see him again for about ten days. Every evening I would go to the window and call him for minutes and minutes. He's the only one who knows the truth, the only witness to everything, and that's why he is so dear to me, so precious. I didn't tell the detectives anything interesting, and I told Richard that I couldn't know if Patrick and the man who raped me the first time were one and the same because I never saw the latter's face, but I didn't think so because Patrick was taller and more athletic. The detectives left and I requested that this subject never again be broached with me or with my son, that the whole episode be considered closed, once and for all. Marty looks at me. I don't know what he wants. I bend down to pet him. He perks up. He is my proud and silent accomplice.

I wake up in the middle of the night for no good reason. I don't turn on the lights but I wait a few minutes in total silence. Then I go back to sleep.

In the morning, his heart is no longer beating, he's dead, he has given up the ghost on the rug beside my bed. Curtains are not enough—the sun is majestic. I get up and close the shutters to maintain a favorable half-light, then I go back to bed. I don't look at him, don't touch him. I just leave him where he is and cry over his departure and all the rest, noiselessly and continuous into midafternoon, my T-shirt and my sheets soaked as if a summer shower had surprised us in the middle of a bad dream.

I no longer have a single tear left when I see to him, scooping him into a hatbox I fished out of the attic, left over from when Irène was twenty. I add a few personal items—a little silver bell, a brush, a rabbit-fur mouse. I bury him at the foot of a tree in the garden.

The phone rings but I don't answer it.

I have taken care of Vincent, supported him, protected him, relieved him of his guilt. I have not forgotten him for a second since it happened. I slept with my bedroom door open for days, so that if something was wrong I would hear it. I also took care of Richard when Hélène dumped him in the spring for a young screenwriter, going out to bars with him for a few drinks when he felt alone and needed to talk. But the remedies I employ for others have no effect on me. My speeches are of no help at all. So strong and so weak.

The next day, I go to the QuickBurger to see my son in his new uniform and I tell him Marty died and he asks me if he went peacefully. But he doesn't look too terribly unhappy in his new position and starts threading through the tables once again, smiling left and right, and yet later on Anna will tell me that he called her after I left to say that I wasn't doing well, that I looked, to use his exact words, "like death warmed over."

Since I'm not too far away, I go visit Irène. My father is lying next to her but I pay no attention. I flower only one half of the grave site and I never speak to him. I pretend he doesn't exist.

"Marty is dead," I say. The sky is so blue you might expect to see palm trees sprouting up all over the place. The cemetery is empty. I last a few minutes. Then my lips begin to tremble, I mumble, and I promptly get out of there. And I can hear her calling after me, "What a chickenshit you turn out to be, darling!"

Anna parks outside my house at dusk. I watch her get out of the car and walk up the path toward me while I rock the glider ever so slightly and it makes a long creaking sound.

It's still very hot and her arms are bare.

"Marty is dead," I say as she walks up.

"Yes, I know," she answers, sitting down next to me. She puts her hand on mine. It's been at least three months since we last touched one another, during which we have had a strictly business relationship. "I was thinking maybe I should rent a room out to a student," I say.

The moon is bright. On the other side of the road, a few hundred feet away, Patrick's house is like a shining toy placed on a silvery lawn. They have mowed it, trimmed the hedges, cleaned the windows, replaced the water heater, but the woman from the agency could turn the place into sugar and gingerbread and I suppose she still couldn't sell it.

"Why don't you rent me the room?" she suggests, never taking her eyes from the view.

"Oh," I say, with the slightest of nods.

TELL THE WORLD THIS BOOK WAS

GOOD	BAD	SO-SO

PHILIPPE DJIAN is the award-winning author of more than twenty novels, including the best seller *37°2 le matin*, published in English as *Betty Blue*. *Elle* is the fifth of his novels to be adapted for the screen. Published in French under its original title "*Oh...*," this best-selling novel received the 2012 Prix Interallié.

MICHAEL KATIMS is a Brooklyn-born screenwriter and translator. He worked with Roman Polanski to bring Yasmina Reza's play to the big screen in *Carnage*, and with Jacques Perrin on the U.S. version of *Oceans*. His subtitling credits include Dany Boon's *Bienvenue chez les Ch'tis* (*Welcome to the Sticks*) and Raymond Depardon's *Les Habitants*.